UNCLE OVID'S EXERCISE BOOK

Illinois State University / Fiction Collective Series

Curtis White, Series Editor

ALSO AVAILABLE IN THE SERIES

Plane Geometry and Other Affairs of the Heart
by R. M. Berry

When Things Get Back to Normal
by Constance Pierce

Griever: An American Monkey King in China
by Gerald Vizenor

UNCLE OVID'S EXERCISE BOOK

Fictions by
DON WEBB

ILLINOIS STATE UNIVERSITY
Normal

FICTION COLLECTIVE
New York · Boulder

This publication is the 1988 winner of the Illinois State
University/Fiction Collective Award, jointly sponsored by the
Illinois State University Fine Arts Festival and the Fiction
Collective.

Published by the Illinois State University/Fiction Collective with
assistance from the Illinois State University Foundation and the
Illinois Arts Council; the support of the Publications Center,
University of Colorado, Boulder; and the cooperation of Brooklyn
College and Teachers & Writers Collaborative.

Publication of this book was also made possible, in part, by public
funds from the National Endowment for the Arts and the New
York State Council on the Arts.

Grateful acknowledgement is made to Zulfikar Ghose for his
permission to use the quotation in Metamorphosis No. 9. This
quotation appears in the Author's Notes to Ghose's *Hulme's
Investigations into the Bogart Script*, Curbstone Press, 1981.

Acknowledgement is also made to *Gamut, Semiotext(e), nrg,* and
Cassandra Anthology, in which parts of this book originally
appeared.

Library of Congress Cataloging in Publication Data.

Webb, Don.
    Uncle Ovid's Exercise Book.

I. Title
PS 3573.E1953U5   1988   813.'54   88-18060
ISBN: 0-932511-17-1
ISBN: 0-932511-18-x (pbk.)'

Manufactured in the United States of America.
Typography by Abe Lerner.
Typesetting by James Kalmbach.

To Rosemary
and to all artists and writers
mentioned explicitly and
implicitly in the text

UNCLE OVID'S EXERCISE BOOK

```
┌─────────────────────────┐
│                         │
│      Uncle Ovid's       │
│      Exercise Book      │
│                         │
└─────────────────────────┘
```

METAMORPHOSIS NO. 1

Eyewake. Caught like Gulliver. Strands of light, blue and red, cover my body. Cabalistic stars at juncture points, gold and silver, like Mrs. Jones, the music teacher, gave.

The lightweb offers no resistance to my movement. I am completely encased, the thickest webbing over my crotch. Can't brush it off. A few strands radiate away from me like dandelion seeds, pointing NNW of my bed.

I roll and stand. As I brush against the sheets, small blue lightning discharges. My tiny bedroom smells of ozone and roses. I catch my reflection from the mirror opposite; I'm lit up like an Xmas tree, complete with ectoplasmic jockstrap.

There's a tug, a strange gravity centered in my solar plexus and just behind my balls. Apparently having netted his catch, the alien fisherman now reels me in.

I pull on a soft gray football jersey. My running shoes cling, merging with the lightweb. The warm, tight pressure on my crotch makes me stiff.

There's a quivering sense of anticipation. I tremble. I remember the first time I mounted Judi Barlowe in the station wagon. Nervous static thick enough to spread like marmalade.

I'm hot. My dick's beginning to lubricate itself. Ants crawl over my head and spine. Formication.

I pace around the flat. I think of calling my boss to say I'll be late for work. I think of prayer. I think of Valium.

The itching tug in my chest grows. I run out the door, past the postman who doesn't even notice I'm the fiber-optic poster child.

Out in the sultry overcast day, I know where to go.

The trees, the street noises, the graffiti, the postal truck all coalesce into a tunnel. At the other end's a park bench.

I begin jogging, running to the park.

I'm at one with my target. I run through the tunnel of blur. Almost intersect a yellow Cadillac. Get off the road, bastard. I've nothing to fear, chance opens a clear space around me.

Running, the lines grow brighter—I am nearing their source. Finally, on dew-covered grass I stand in front of the bench.

It is mottled green and brown from previous paintings. On its upper right corner is a red spray-paint trident, the Hebrew letter *shin*, which corresponds to fire. I think of Liberace's candelabra.

I tear off my shorts. My dick hard, glowing—bright blue. I fall on the bench, begin fucking a knothole.

The knothole changes to sweet pink cunt. A polyp tunnel grasping me tightly all the way up my shaft. Its warm wetness splatting against my balls.

I fuck the bench, ramming it like my first piece of brown boy ass. Its rough cunt so tight that each thrust I see silver spots of pleasurepainpleasure in front of my eyes. The wood is crumbling under my nails. The lightweb burns brighter and brighter,

each line an orgasm burning into my skin.
The film comes to a jerky stop. You and I are alone in a smelly downtown porn theater, surrounded by metal folding chairs. The frame melts, starting with the *shin* and spreading outwards. First brown, then amber, then white = pure information. Now the show can begin. The theater is on fire.

METAMORPHOSIS NO. 2

Hector Steelpoint, who thought of himself as one vast pulsating interpenetrating particular but whose neighbors thought of him as the ol' strumpot, has begun a certain disintegration of character since his hypnotherapy. The hypnotherapy—purchased at the American Hypnogogic Scientific Institute whose advertisements haunt late night electromagnetic media between Crazy Lou's Car Lot and timely reminders not to create forest fires—is guaranteed to help clients break the chains of addictive behavior, in Hector's case the late night feeding of the strumpot, maintaining its great white roundness.

The therapy consisted of Hector's being hypnotized in a Naugahyde recliner while the hypnotist droned on about the tastelessness of food and Hector's new self-image. Think thin to be thin. A cassette recording of the spiel (or spell?) replayed everyday would drive the new programming deep into Hector's core. Unfortunately for Hector his therapist had eaten that day at Tandor's House of Indian Cuisine and was in need of gastric relief. During the hypnosis the therapist dropped two effervescent tablets into a water-filled shot glass and drank the bubbling mixture during strategic pauses in his monologue.

The effervescent sound and sizzling image wedded itself to the concept of weight loss in Hector. Leaving the therapy session he became light of step, bubbly with enthusiasm.

That night—and subsequent nights as he used the autohypnosis drill to bring on sleep—Hector dreamed of vast Hector-shaped Alka Seltzer tablets boiling away. The bubbles were Hector-shaped as well, tiny excess Hectors.

Hector soon discovered that household tasks—dishes, garbage, bathroom scrubbing—completed themselves as he slept. Like the Grimm brothers' shoemaker, he had been blessed by elves laboring in the night. An early morning piss revealed the truth: his elves were industrious little Hectors finishing the business of the day. $d(Hector) / dy$

The classroom where he taught high school science also benefited from this miniscule work crew. Although he never saw them, the evidence of their work in completed computer grade forms and gleaming test tubes was indisputable.

Paradoxically, Hector didn't feel less energetic as he was diminished, but more so. Light of foot, clear of mind. The only drawback was the loss of certain memories, tastes, and opinions. Often he would pause, having lost a word, a phrase, or a whole idea—like the Second Law of Thermodynamics. His students didn't notice (or, strictly speaking, they did, but believed anyone over forty to be senile anyway). These losses seemed minor to Hector compared to having conquered the life-long problem of fat.

Summer came at last and Hector looked forward to a strong physical season, which mounds of sweaty flesh had always denied him. It was during the summer that Hector disappeared.

The neighbors say that the new, thin, handsome Hector ran off with a stewardess to the Bahamas.

However, if you're born with the caul as I am and walk past Hector's old house, sometimes you'll see fat little elves trimming the hedge or cleaning the gutter, elves who look remarkably like the ol' strumpot.

METAMORPHOSIS NO. 3

The February sunlight changed the spring water to urine in Dr. Plotner's decoctions. Spiking the prisoner's drinks with mescaline and filling logbooks for dark men with double lightning bolt insignia while dreamers in Berlin seek the chimera of Total Control, mirror image of the philosopher's stone.

Dr. Plotner returns to his measurements with a dreamy expression . . .

The guards select a subject, an "intellectual" Dr. Plotner had said. (A disgusting term applied to a Jew.) A middle-aged rabbi. Abram Virag, a student of the Kabbala and a translator of the *Midrash*.

Abram expects death as they hustle him through the gates of Dr. Plotner's fenced-off complex. The last few weeks had been the "aviation" series and the screams had penetrated into the dusty exercise yards.

Abram sits waiting in a small room warmer than any place he's been in months. Warm sweet tea the everpresent swastika flag isolation.

Dr. Plotner enters with a smile and a notebook. Hands Abram the notebook. Write an essay on camp life. The Doctor sits across from him writing an essay of his own with frequent references to his wristwatch.

Abram doesn't question. He writes—in Yiddish, perhaps a small act of defiance—and drinks tea. The colors sharpen in the room, become unbearably intense. Abram is distracted by motion in the window. Someone dancing in the camp. Dancing?

A green tall warty man dancing freely. Dancing with gold and blue lights rising out of the ground. The Gestapo ignores him.

The Doctor looks different—his face flat and Aztec, his pen an obsidian blade.

The dancing man wears a talisman, the ten-orbed Tree of

Life. A fellow Kabbalist. His eyes deep and gold like gems from the walls of Solomon's temple.

The walls of the room shrink away from Abram. He stands with the dancing man outside the building.

Mescalito points at the building. Abram turns and the February sunlight becomes amber. Abram picks up a lump of amber containing Dr. Plotner, a dark segmented insect.

He follows the dancing man from the camp.

METAMORPHOSIS NO. 4

The flesh becoming stale and crystallizing. The eyes fixing. A sluggish jelling of the internal organs brought on by too many injections of arsenic. Mr. Gneiss realizes that his career as side show exhibit has gone the way of the hunger artist.

No one believes in him anymore. His heavy, slow movements convince the rubes that he is an automaton and a cheap automaton at that—one of very few moving parts. Blue-eyed midwestern farmers who pay the two bits extra to lay a hand on his petrified chest mutter "plaster o' paris."

Lately the marks have been demanding their money back. Partly it's Mr. Blake's fault—buying the five-legged sheep and other papier-mâché grotesqueries has cheapened the show, robbed it of its class as an all-human show. Partly it's the death of the Bearded Lady and the departure of Col. Louis Lilliput to Hollywood for that Oz film. But partly it is because of Mr. Gneiss's new immobile state.

He knows that Mr. Blake intends to leave him behind as one discards any object which is no longer useful. In the night he hears the trucks loaded—no one comes to help him into his trailer. The caravan starts its motors and Mr. Gneiss begins to turn but they will be impossibly far down the road—even perhaps out of sight—by the time he scans the eastern-bound highway.

Early in the morning the desert wind rises blowing sharp fine red sand. Mr. Gneiss begins the long process of erosion . . . .

METAMORPHOSIS NO. 5

Marco Phillips was born under the sign of the Second Banana or, as they say in the Texas Hemisphere, The Sidekick. So when it came to pass that W.B. Porter, the Last of the Singing Cowboys, was to be born in San Antone, Marco moseyed over to San Antone to wait. And W.B. was born and wrapped in swaddling clothes from Neiman Marcus. W.B. was too small to need a sidekick, so Marco was placed in temporal stasis at the Armadillo Self Storage.

After W.B. got his degree in Chemical Engineering from Rice University, he rode off on his Palomino to San Antone and revived Marco. There was some trouble with the bill. Who foots the bill for storage, the cowboy or the sidekick? It's not in *Cowboy Etiquette*. But finally W.B. paid. W.B. smiled and the gleam of the smile burned the smog off of the city. And as W.B. and Marco were riding out of the city, the Mayor of San Antone rode up in his Cadillac and gave the boys the key to the city on account of the smog removal. And W.B. said, "Shucks, 'tweren't nothing."

And Marco and W.B. rode out into the mesas. They camped beneath a beautiful Texas sunset. Marco began the beans and the sourdough and W.B. began to yodel. He yodeled better than the Yodeling Kid from Pine Ridge. The spirits of Tom Mix and Gene Autrey drew near.

After the meal W.B. said he needed to go into the scrub alone. Now, all Texans know what it means when you go off to the bushes. But Marco felt a strange urge to follow W.B. A man's

15

got to trust his hunches.

So Marco sneaked down the mesa through the mesquite and the soapberry and the yucca. And he came upon a strange golden glow. Marco crawled on his belly like an Injun scout. Through a cedar he saw Varuna and Vishnu and Hathor and all the other cow gods and goddesses and they was givin' W.B. a mission. Marco knew W.B. was the cowboy he'd waited for. Marco creeped back to camp real quiet like.

The Mendoza gang was riding into El Paso. They were tough hombres schooled in the Fourteen Mysteries of Toltec Sorcery and besides they packed laser-targeting Uzis. Nobody knew what the Mendozas wanted. But W.B. and Marco felt the call and rode through the night

Krishna was also favored by the cow gods. His name means "dark" or "stained." He had the divine power and it could rub off. Many demons gained salvation by Krishna's touch in combat. Many shepherds' daughters achieved salvation (not to mention prolonged orgasms) by Krishna's lovemaking. Some people hope Krishna's divinity will rub off on them if they chant his name long enough.

Laura Enfield put down the Krishna book. She decided the shepherds' daughters had the best idea. She went to her Avon products. She would be ready when W.B. rode into town.

Twenty minutes after dawn W.B. and Marco rode in. Marco's chestnut gelding's hide was black with sweat, but W.B.'s Palomino stallion seemed bright and fresh. The boys stopped at a Winchell's for doughnuts. The counterman said,

"Y'all just ride in?"

Marco said, "We heard the call. We came from the badlands."

The doughnutman didn't seem to hear.

Marco said, "From the *malpaís,* the alkali flats, the poverty flats, the wasteland, the filth land, the barrens."

The doughnutman still didn't notice.

W.B. said, "Yep."

The doughnutman said, "Oh, what'll you have?"

Marco learned Second Banana Rule No. Twenty-Seven, "No one listens to the sidekick."

There's a corollary to this rule that doesn't occur in this story, so I'm passing it along for your information: "They listen to the sidekick if he's forming a rescue party for the boss." I could've created a situation for that rule to show up, but I reckoned you'd want the story just like it happened. Natural like.

*

The Mendoza gang ate at a Coco's. After breakfast they scanned the papers. Rico spotted it, an article on developers pouring a lot of money into houses and condos north of Houston. Rico read the article aloud. The Mendozas laughed. They would ride to Houston and hijack those big mixer trucks full of money ready for pouring. They would drive them like cattle across the Mexican border and pour the money into money-hungry Mexico. Fausto, the *jefe,* twirled his mustachios with delight. "Genaro," he said, "ride over to the Exxon station and buy us a map showing how to get to Houston."

*

The boys enjoyed their coffee and doughnuts while the doughnutman went to the back to call Laura Enfield. He said, "W.B. Porter came in this morning. He and the little guy plan to shoot it out with the Mendoza gang and after the shootout the

17

boys will light out to the barrens."

Laura said, "The alkali flats?"

The doughnutman said, "Yeah. So you better be quick."

Laura said, "Thanks, Al, I owe you one." Laura dialed up Rosa. There were pleasantries and then Laura said, "Rosa, I need a favor. Could you warn Fausto that W.B. hit town?"

"*Sí.* But why?"

"I want Fausto to ride on so I can have W.B. to myself."

"Consider it done."

Fausto studied the map. He marked an X between Houston and Conroe. F.M. 1960. He called upon the first of the Fourteen Mysteries and the wind cloaked the Mendozas from human eyes and ears. Just as W.B. and Marco left the Winchell's, the wind blew off Marco's Stetson. The wind spooked the horses.

W.B. sang and calmed the horses. The boys rode to the Holiday Inn where the Mendozas were last seen. W.B. kicked open the door.

The suite was empty except for Laura and a king-size bed.

"You better wait outside. There may be trouble," W.B. told Marco.

"Do not hasten to bid me adieu," said Laura.

But W.B. kept on buttoning his shirt and smiling his prairie smile.

"Remember the Red River Valley and the cowgirl that loved you so true." Laura's geography was weak but her heart was in the right place.

But W.B. wouldn't look back for he knew Laura had tipped off the Mendozas.

Marco was cooling his feet in the pool.

W.B. said, "Git your boots on. We've got to ride to Houston."

∗

Several hours earlier, the Mendoza gang arrived at F.M. 1960 and IH-45. They let their horses graze on the highway right-of-way and Genaro climbed up a ponderosa pine to spot a mixer truck.

Rico asked Fausto, "When we get the money to Mexico what will we do?"

Fausto said, "Find a pocket of poverty and let it pour—after taking fifty percent for handling."

"What will you do with your share?"

"I will get my Uzi silver-plated except for the notch."

"The notch?"

"*Sí*. The notch I will carve when I shoot W.B. Porter, Last of the Singing Cowboys."

From high above came a voice, "I've spotted two mixers."

The mixers were headed for the Twin Oak Heights development. Fausto called forth the second of the Fourteen Mysteries, an Invocation of Ah Puk, god of death, paperwork, and fake IDs. Small bright plastic badges appeared on the Mendozas' shirts. The Mendozas saddled up and rode across country to the Twin Oak Heights development office.

As the Mendozas rode in they fired their automatic weapons into the air and cried out, "*'Riba, 'riba!*" The developers took fright and fled the development in Toyotas, Datsuns, and Nissan pickups.

The Mendozas had just hidden their Uzis when the mixer trucks drove in.

The trucks stopped. One of the drivers swung out and approached Fausto.

The driver didn't like the sombrero or the mustachios or the bandoliers, but relaxed when he saw the kelly green badge. The driver said, "You're Mr. Meyer?"

"*Sí*. Why don't you have coffee with my men?"

"Don't got time. Show us where to pour the stuff."

"My men will do the pouring."

"How are we supposed to get back to Houston?"

"Rico—er, eh, Bill, get these men some horses."

"I ain't gointa take—"

"—You see this badge. You know what it means?"

The driver knew. The two drivers saddled up while Fausto signed the invoice for two-and-a-half tons of money-slurry.

*

"*Jefe*, we've got two trucks, let's head home before W.B. Porter and Marco catch up with us."

"Are you kidding? There's lots more where this came from. Besides, I have a plan."

Fausto dipped a ladleful of money from a mixer. He rode to a nearby Dairy Queen. Soon its marquee read, "Welcome W.B. Porter."

*

W.B. and Marco rode out of El Paso. Hours later Laura Enfield would follow them in a VW Microbus.

At the outskirts of Houston the boys saw two greenhorns trying to ride two beautiful Arabians. W.B., whose mind is as Clear as the Light of the Void, suspected something was wrong. He called out, "Whoa! Where you boys headed with those two fine horses?"

"Not much of anywhere, mister. Know where we can rent a horse trailer?"

"Why'd greenhorns like you come riding anyway?"

"We didn't do this on purpose. We delivered our trucks to the development and they said they'd do their own pouring and gave us these horses as loaners."

"Cement trucks?"

"No sir. Money trucks."

"And these 'developers'—did they wear sombreros?"

"Yep."

"Which way is this development?"

The greenhorns pointed. W.B. and Marco rode off.

A mile further down the road was the Dairy Queen. The boys almost passed it.

"Can't pass up a genuine Texas welcome," W.B. said. So they dismounted and Marco hitched their horses to the picnic tables.

"Look girls, it's W.B. Porter. Won't you sing for us, Mr. Porter?"

A singing cowboy can never turn down a fan. It's the Code of the West. So W.B. unslung his guitar and a stage appeared. W.B. sang.

He sang the songs of Gene Autrey and Tom Mix and Buck Jones and Roy Rogers. He sang the old ballads, the new ballads, and the ballads of middling age. A day and a night and a day passed. W.B. unslung his sitar and began to sing the hymns of the Gopastami or Cow Festival, the most sacred cowboy hymns.

Laura burst into the Dairy Queen and leapt on stage. "Still your sacred sitar!" she cried, "Look at your audience!"

W.B. looked. Except for Marco they were all wearing Walkmans. He'd been duped. W.B. and Marco ran to their horses. W.B. shot a last look of gratitude and desire Laura's way. As he looked upon her lithe form he thought of *boopis* or "cow-eyed" the adjective used by Homer to describe the divine Hera. But he said nothing, there wasn't time for mushy stuff.

During W.B.'s stay at the Dairy Queen, the Mendozas had acquired sixteen mixer trucks.

The Mendozas were headed for Laredo. W.B. and Marco set off at once. W.B. cautioned Laura not to follow. It would be too

21

dangerous.

Laura caught a plane out of Houston Hobby. Unfortunately, Fausto had guessed that Laura would be the loyal type. Alberto and Juan nabbed her at the Laredo International Airport. The Mendozas had parked the mixers in two rows of eight near the Rio Grande. They would cross here where there was no bridge. No one would find this spot. They would use sorcery. Fausto invoked the third of the Fourteen Mysteries. The Rio Grande left its banks and hovered like a glistening lasso in the air. It was moving north, taking the border of Mexico with it. When it touched down the sixteen trucks would be safely in Mexico.

Six shots rang out.

W.B. had shot the bottom of the floating river. There was a cloudburst. The Rio Grande splashed over the Mendozas. The water flowed back to its natural boundaries, leaving the trucks and the gang on the U.S. side. Only the *jefe* Fausto had been prepared for this contingency. He laughed from beneath his umbrella.

Fausto said, "Gringo, if you come any closer your woman will die." He had his Uzi right against Laura's silken neck.

W.B. said, "I'm sure Laura understands the need for certain sacrifices."

Laura's expression showed clearly she did not understand the need. Fausto shrugged and said, "Plan Two."

Rico led a yearling out from behind a truck. Fausto pointed his gun at the cow and said, "If you don't drop your gun, amigo, it's veal-time!"

W.B. was shocked. The words of the third-century *Mahabhrata* came to mind, "All that kill, eat, or *permit* the slaughter of cows rot in hell for as many years as there are hairs on the body of the cow so slain." It looked like a pretty hairy yearling. W.B. dropped his guns. Marco dismounted and began to drop his guns.

Laura tripped Fausto. He fell forward, a rain of gunfire fortunately missing the sacred cow. Marco shot the falling bandit chief. W.B. retrieved his six-shooters. The Mendozas took aim and discovered that their Uzis wouldn't fire.

W.B. and Marco had the drop on them. The Texas Rangers arrived and carted away the Mendozas. The Houston development money was safe.

In gratitude for his works, the cow gods and goddesses transformed W.B. Porter into a giant saguaro cactus. Every day he meditates in vegetable bliss, luxuriating in sunlight. He guards the border and his brow is wreathed by flowers in the spring.

Marco and Laura married and lived happily ever after. Sometimes they picnic near W.B.

METAMORPHOSIS NO. 6

The flattening had begun with the tearing down of Flying Gothic cathedrals. It had progressed with the equating of men with animals by Darwin. Perhaps the arts achieved their greatest pancaking when Le Corbusier proclaimed all doorways would be thin golden rectangles—finally the fisheye lens

Tomas stops typing his paper on "Flattening of Perception" for Art 351. The coffee in the brown Melmac cup proclaims its staleness with rainbow film. Cold coffee old coffee better than no coffee.

Tomas leaves the desk to sink into the tired yellow bean bag chair. When he closes his eyes, his paper's theme summons up dances of paper dolls—he wishes that his professors could be as easily crumpled and discarded. Tomas pictures Dr. Faustroll unrolling in the water like toilet paper. Should he mention the Duo-Dimension spell from "Dungeons and Dragons," or would Dr. Blake see that reference as too helplessly pop?

In the physics class he failed last semester there had been an equation about flattening as you approach the speed of light.

Don Webb

Lorentz-Fitzgerald. Attributed to pressure from the ether—always meant to tell mother, when flying face the front of the plane because then you're thinner.

The Duo-Dimension spell enables an M-U to become as thin as a sheet of paper—no, thinner really, thin as an idealized plane. Corbu would've loved that—no doorways, just mail drops.

A stomach grumbling pulls Tomas away from speculations. After checking a depressingly empty fridge Tomas heads out. Carefully he passes through the crack between door and wall.

METAMORPHOSIS NO. 7

Gradually his face has come to resemble the face in the photo he found in the park. His jaws ached for weeks—they were elongating, giving him the crocodile jaws of the photo. His hair began to lighten from dishwater to true blond.

The photo had been taped to an elm. It was just above eye level. He couldn't say why he kept it. Perhaps the summer scene in the background appealed to him on coat-wrapped Groundhog Day.

The change in eye color was pleasing. Photoman had hazel eyes with gold flecks—like opal chips floating in glycerine. Far more desirable than faded blue.

The new-found tan brought favorable comments around the office.

The photoman dressed better than he. On impulse he began to acquire the GQ look.

A week after his jaws stopped hurting—on April 30—he went to the park again. A sad-faced brunette hung around the tree.

Her face. He recognized her—she was the woman in the photo.

24

She was looking his way. Her face filled with longing. "I've missed you so much, Mary. Let's go home."

METAMORPHOSIS NO. 8

Rarified dewy dawn piercing and clean as a scalpel. Paul wades through the grass in a pleasant fugue, scenes of tomorrow's closing replayed from last year and superimposing themselves on this perfect morning. Aspens' golden hissing. Locking the cabin's doors, scaring a lone white-tail deer upward on a loose shale ridge, emptying the Coke bottle and copper tubing hummingbird feeders of their red syrup and stacking them in overpainted white cabinets.

The last trip of the season is always Paul's. Everyone else hates closing. Cold, lists of trivial actions to be filled and crossed off. Paul loves it. The tight bundle of self can be unraveled a little so garbage can be chucked and treasures shined.

Paul passes the gray warped wood shack built as a worker's shelter during the big logging of forty years ago. A sharp picture from childhood rises. Drinking hot cumin-spiced pumpkin soup, visiting Uncle Hassan in Tangiers.

The incongruity stopped him. Tangiers? Uncle Hassan? No Tangiers, no Uncle Hassan. Paul decides altitude and old age must be getting to him. He smells—imagines smelling—hashish.

No. From the shed. Paul enters the slanting doorhole. On the cold rotten wood floor lies a pipe, smoking.

Paul sees the tiny shed empty but for the pipe. He pulls outside; no one on the roof. Only one furrow through the waist-high grass.

Paul returns. Picks up the hot pipe carefully, as though a snake.

25

A small dark pellet with a glowing ring expanding from a white ash center. The pipe is about six inches long, red and blue enameled Britannia metal. The mouthpiece is polished through years of use.

Paul takes a long slow drag. Soon the sun will leave the sky and he will unroll his rug and recite the first Sura. He draws his *jellaba* about him and walks into the dusty marketplace.

METAMORPHOSIS NO. 9

Succeeding sentences, the second explicitly or implicitly refer- ring to the content of the first (and so on until the text is pre- sumed to be completed), give us the impression of a continuing reality. But they are only sentences, one after the other, each itself and only itself. And grammar? All prestidigitation em- ploys rules.

The above is the near-epigraph to Zulfikar Ghose's *Hulme's Investigations into the Bogart Script*. Near because Mr. Ghose could not track down the source of the quotation and wished to avoid using an anonymous epigraph. There are two possible sources for the text:

One: Zulfikar Ghose possessed of clairlexia (the reading of what is not yet written or is far away) read it in *Uncle Ovid's Exercise Book*.

Two: (This is the most acceptable.) Zulfikar Ghose heard the voice in a dream. One may always trust voices spoken by an invisible presence, if the voice is clear and the presence is radiant. The words after all form one of the Keys of Dreams, which are given to many writers from Ovid to Sheila Ascher. It is the simplest metamorphosis of all—letting sentences change each other into writing.

Everyone knows this trick. You are using it yourself right

now. What you don't realize is that the words of *Uncle Ovid's* aren't normal words. I bought them from an adept in the Andes. After they slip through Broca's area of your brain they pass into the bloodstream. They echo down long arterial corridors. They nudge messenger RNA. Even now they are triggering your metamorphosis—that mutation you've been trying to avoid. Darwin and Stephen Jay Gould don't know about this kind of evolution.

Or perhaps I'm lying. Perhaps these are regular words.

Yonder lies de palace of my fadder de Caliph.

METAMORPHOSIS NO. 10

In the sun at noon Radiant Heat Monopoly with a wriggle stood naked (every gun throbbing) bare feet in dog's excrement screen and came out repeat performance page quivering with incoordination.

Hard-faced matron neared the boundary shock when your neck breaks. The Mongolian controllers room you are already must be in Lhasa; his leg, his cock flipped delicate as watches burning insect wings.

Radiant Heat Monopoly stands naked in front of his gay bar the Sun. In his right hand a spherical ruby—synthetic, the size of a goose egg. In his left hand his erect cock.

Across the asphalt was Ix Tab patroness of those who hang themselves. She held a hemp rope and a vial of rancid jissim collected from a thousand hung men.

The Old Ones in semi-mirrored cylinders deep in Lhasa made silent wagers.

Semi-visible sepia fans, ghostly watchers of ancient Western films. The acrid smell of decaying celluloid and stale popcorn hung in the air.

27

Radiant Heat Monopoly waits for the solstice sunlight to rise above his bar striking his laser gem. Seconds away the red light would blossom forth and sear his ancient opponent.

Ix Tab slowly spins her noose. At the right moment she will throw it lasso-like collecting the thousand and first specimen. The laserlight appears—his aim is off by twenty or more centimeters. She swings her noose outward catching the golden neck of Radiant Heat Monopoly. His neck cracks with the sound of dry reeds.

His body pitches forward onto the gravel. His cock spurts forth creamy jissim glittering in the sun.

Ix Tab catches the gelatinous mass in her vial. The phantom fans return to ectoplasmic showings of *High Noon*.

Ix Tab quaffs the vial. She believes it to be the Medicine of Metals. The strings of rancid jissim glide gaggingly down her throat.

A convection wave flows through her. In the swimming air of summer she blurs out of focus.

The air suddenly becomes clear. Radiant Heat Monopoly stands grins and drops empty vial and noose.

Stepping over his used body he returns to his bar.

A distant chuckle comes from a fresh shiny cylinder kilometers underground in Lhasa.

METAMORPHOSIS NO. 11

Officially, Comte de Lautreamont, author of *Maldrodor*, and Comte d'Erlette, author of *Cultes des Goules*, died on the same day in 1870. On the day before their official deaths, each received a small stoppered bottle by mail. The bottles bore no return address. Each contained an oily greenish fluid. The bottles gave an overwhelming impression of *antiquity*.

The counts rode all night. At dawn they met on the Mediterranean coast near Marseille. They dismissed their weeping servants. They walked hand-in-hand into the sea. When the water reached their thighs, they removed the bottles from their vests and quaffed the potions.

It tasted of absinthe. They had been deceived. They turned to leave when the pain struck. They were right after all. Their bowels burst through their skin. Their arms and heads were sucked into their torsos. Their genitals traveled upward toward the emptying abdomens. Their guts turned inside out.

They had become octopi with silken skin and four hundred suckers. The great Cthulu had rewarded his messengers.

They spent ten years among the drowned ruins of the Mediterranean, occasionally feasting on the succulent flesh of mariners. Then they swam to the cold mineral-rich waters of the North Atlantic. They were honored at the city of the Deep Ones, whose walls are mother-of-pearl.

They traveled through marine tunnels to the bottomless lakes near Sauk City, Wisconsin. There they colored the dreams of the Arkham House writers—producing many eldritch tomes bound in black Novolex.

Of late they have dwelt in the Red Sea. In Africa famine has erased the line between waking and dreaming. In Africa the Old Ones will acquire enough of the dream stuff to break through again. When the stars are right they will re-form, and R'lyeh will rise from the watery depths.

The Old Ones will be formed of Africa's hunger and long-imprisoned Cthulu's rage. They will seek out the fatter and greener lands.

It is unpleasant to live in a seaside town or to smell the filth of the sea. There is fear in the lapping of the water. I shall move to the highest mountain.

landscape like a pizza (especially with the red glow of the Bessemer Towers) so he bites it breaking miles of strata bursting houses farms fields. He chews with earth running down his unshaven jowls. Small men and women run from whole and demolished structures screaming at the destruction and the death.

He wipes the blood and earth and molten steel off his chin. Leaves the room. He walks down right and right again an L-shaped hall with parquet floors. He pauses at the cooler to wash the last bit of earth down his throat. He removes a tiny bloody skull from between his cheek and gum, sets it on the drain of the water fountain; it is barely large enough to avoid anonymity by falling through the grate. Further down the halls he fancies that overhead fluorescents dim just perceptibly as he passes beneath.

Finally at an oaken door a brass plate with his therapist's name, Dr. Hurlburt. Cold static arcs between his hand and the knob (accumulated from the action of his boots on the floor varnish).

The receptionist's pale face is lit by the reflection from the glossy paper in front of her from the desk lamp, her sun. She's a refugee from a UFA film. The pale washed-out blue eyes signal him on into the inner office, betraying impatience at his late arrival.

The inner office is darkly paneled, Dr. Hurlburt pursuing a thoughtful expression. The man lies on the green overstuffed leather (vinyl?) couch. The Doctor consults his notes, switches on the tiny imported recorder and begins.

—I believe last time we were discussing a recurrent dream of yours since childhood.

—Yeah, like I'm twelve it's early morning everything still dewy and cold and sparkly. I'm supposed to be feeding chickens but—

Memory is lifting its rosy fingers of dawn.

—but I gotta crap see. I got this terrible pressure in my guts so I go to the outhouse—two holer it was, doc, real luxury—but about twelve feet away I see this rosy cloud—pink mist like cotton candy—all ropy and movin'—

The Doctor recognizes the face seen in the sky many years ago. After the earthquake released gallons of molten iron. Giant unshaven face in the sky the day his parents died. He begins to reach ever so slowly for the blaster in the top right drawer of his dark mahogany desk.

—so I stop and watch it. Like I still need to crap y'see but this's more innaresting. It shoots across the sky right over the outhouse. And these ice madonnas little ice marys just like in Charles Fort's Spain hail down on the outhouse. Bust the old rotten wood to flinders. And I'm about twelve feet away being hit by splinters and glass and old shit—

The Doctor has removed the blaster and is taking aim.

—and I like it see, the stuff just passes right through me and my bowels suddenly let go—

ZAP. Good clean shot. Got most of the couch too. There'll be a spot of trouble collecting the fee from his relatives.

METAMORPHOSIS NO. 13

I. During Holy Week

—A—

It was the week of Easter. She brought home her tangerines and endive, the thought of meat long since gone. She had lost thirty pounds of ugly oily fat. She grew daily more beautiful, more transparent. Her flesh has become exceedingly delicate: random dust motes cut her to the bone.

On Holy Saturday she began to fast to celebrate the Resurrection of the Light. The carrots lying on the octagonal dining

31

table fibrous, grotesque. Food is so dross—a sticky hindrance to luminous beings. Soon she will feed on electric light.

On Monday she began to change into mother-of-pearl inlayed in her bedroom screen. And into abalone earrings on her nightstand. And into the iridescent flakes in her nail polish. The whole of her apartment glowed with a small lunar light.

On Wednesday his keys opened the door. He came with a bouquet of flowers, an offering to take the place of his absence. On the table were moldering endive and rusting tangerines.

He looked everywhere but could not find her. Yet the air held her perfume. He turns the bedroom lights on—and the vanity lights. He showers.

He lays naked and glistening on the bed. He falls asleep, his body lifts six inches above the bed, his cock becomes hard.

He dissolves into light.

—B—

It was the week of tangerines and endive. Easter brought home her thought of meat and thirty pounds of ugly oily fat long since gone. She had lost had become more beautiful exceedingly delicate. Her flesh has become random dust motes and transparent bones. Cut.

She began to fast to celebrate the Light. On Holy Saturday, Resurrection. The octagonal dining table dross sticky feed on electric light. The carrots were lying to her. Never trust a root. "Fibrous," they said, "Grotesque." Soon she will be a luminous being. Hindrance.

On Monday she inlayed her bedroom, her nightstand, and the whole of lunar light. The screen began to change into mother-of-pearl, no abalone earrings. And into iridescent flakes in her nails. Her small apartment glowed with polish.

On Wednesday, bouquet of flowers, absence and tangerines. His keys opened the door. He came with an offering to take the place of his table. Moldering endive and rusting absence. The flat smelled of fresh bread.

He inhaled deeply the random dust motes the ambient light

the last traces of her perfume. He stifled a cry wanting to keep all of her in his lungs.

In his long absence she had succumbed to the curse of Narcissus. And starved in hope of a greater beauty into the thin airs of anorexia.

He closed the door and bolted it and went to the circular bed of their long-forgotten congresses.

In the lotus position he began the slow exhaling not only of the air but of himself. Carefully molecule by molecule he added himself to her airy self. A pink cloud poured from his nostrils. Like a djinn it coalesced. She reformed as he diminished.

In a few moments it is done. Naked and thin they embrace each other in a final lovemaking for neither has the substance to leave the bed and become part of the world of action ever again. The process of becoming a memory.

—C—

I've got to get hold of myself. Spent all week doing nothing except feeding Fiji (God, that cat food is beginning to smell good) and writing perverse little-girl fantasies in my diary. "They'll find this when I'm dead and they'll be so sorry they weren't sweet to me."

I played up the anorexia theme 'cause Paul accused me of having tendencies before we broke up. My original plan was a Holy Week fast plus night visits to the tanning studio—nobody seems to be using it during the holidays—and show up at his class slim and nut-brown.

I think it would have been a stunning entrance. Would've taken Paul's mind off that thick-thighed Romanian with the big boobs. Magda the milkmaid or whatever her name is. But my stubborn body refused to shed the weight. I'll look my best at 81 or 82 but the scale seems stuck at 95. I've even cut out the endive (no big loss. Yech). I see my writing was prophetic—the endive is moldering and the tangerines rusting.

—D—

The grace of God has descended upon me. Since this afternoon His Light is everywhere. Shining in my bones like the fluorescent lights of the English building and every object has a halo. It was as though I caught *light* the way a log catches fire. I'll nap then take out the garbage. Under my mirror a small bright icon of the illuminated girl.

—E—

The excitement of reaching and surpassing my goal (I'm 79 pounds now. Praise God!) has left me weak-kneed. I wish I had a calendar watch 'cause I'm not sure how long I've slept. Wouldn't do to show up at the English building when everybody's at Church. I think it's early Saturday morning but I'm too embarrassed to call Time and Temperature to find out.

In my mirror the face of Gabriel—that is, if Gabriel were a girl instead of a boy angel—on her way to tell Mary the Good News.

Paul will probably order that fat gypsy to leave his classroom and never darken his doorstep again.

I'll rest for awhile.

II. A Late Night Excursion

About ten minutes to closing Paul Kagan realized life would be easier with his tongue removed. He'd admitted to still owning keys to Linda's apartment. Marta insisted that he march over to Linda's flat and return them.

Paul had protested the hour—it was already officially Easter Sunday; his drunken condition—he was frankly finding it difficult to navigate to and from the restroom; and his companion—after all, Marta was "the other woman."

Marta, aided by the clarity of brandy, equated the return of the keys and Paul's true love.

In the ten minutes before Warmetod Pub would close, Paul had opted for a new strategy. He bought six brandy stingers—

three for himself and three for Marta. He hoped they would either render him incapable or deliquesce Marta's equation.

Eleven minutes and a burning stomach later Paul and Marta lurched toward Linda's apartment. There were two pauses. First at the greening statue of the campus's founder where Paul vomited, second at the corner of Braswell and Hawthorne Streets when Marta realized they were several blocks off-course.

It was three o'clock when they stumbled up to the six-story building in the student ghetto. Linda's lights were on.

The chill night air and lengthy walk had produced in Paul a state approaching equilibrium. He commanded Marta to wait on the stoop and resolutely made for the elevator.

The elevator was slower than the stairs and enabled him to rehearse his entrance. Saw the lights on, thought I'd check in. See you Monday. Etc.

He'd leave the keys dangling in her doorknob in case Marta later went through his pockets.

There was no answer to his light knock. He unlocked the door and went in.

The flat smelled of fresh bread, mildewed lettuce and rotten tangerines. Every light in the place was on. It seemed the light had been concentrated in its confinement. He swam through a medium of light to the bedroom.

On the disarrayed circular bed, the only thing approximating new furniture in Linda's apartment, was a green leather diary. He began to read:

—F—

. . . On the table were moldering endives and tangerines. Marta, meanwhile, spurred on by coldness and a full bladder, had silently entered the apartment behind him. The thick light settled all around her. The light. . .

Paul tossed the diary and turned. Marta stood in the living

room a dreamy smile on her lips a bright eerie light shining from her eyes.

METAMORPHOSIS NO. 14

The old wooden school building (some correspondence and constellation of all evil signs), the buckling juxtaposition of old gas stations, laundromats, frozen custard booths and all the dreary artifacts of an earlier era explode out of that evidence that we had consciously overlooked . . . .

Corbu's Radiant City was finally built in 2020. Clean gleaming glass towers reflecting each other and a purity of aesthetic unknown to earlier architecture. Located seven kilometers from the glassy ruins of New Orleans, the new symmetric complex would have been the Mississippi's gateway to the Gulf if that august river still flowed.

Its inhabitants were chosen by lot from the survivors— mostly the rural population of Southern Texas and Louisiana— by the Provisional People's Government. The "lucky few" were not overjoyed by the spotless dustless miles of glass and steel, but considering the alternative proposed by the Provisional Government . . . .

Two great towers dominated the City. Administration and Police. The Police tower was especially feared for the purist architects of the City had declared that the golden glass rectangles would not be marred by curtains. By coincidence every residential unit could be watched from the Police tower. Just as every work unit could be visually monitored from Administration.

Each citizen, let us be kind, citizen filled his day with twelve golden hours, Horace would have been pleased, a veritable hive of the Golden Mean, a golden light flicking on in the Department of Urine each time each made golden water, in their hearts they knew they were right, everyone could see that in the golden reflection from the towers. Every citizen.

Mardi Gras memories had gone with the hard gammas. No evil dark signs now. The grid parsed everything too closely. No bad cultures could grow in such tiny cells.

There were sports and food and plug-ins and sex and a twenty four hour broadcast of giant mutant crayfish battling in the corrosive slime of the Mississippi. Ruled space had defeated muddy barefooted time. But there is still darkness in the bright space of air around everything.

Some mutant spider, engendered by the radiation or the viruses of the decades before, began weaving a vast web between the two towers. Glistening with dew, each morning its ropy arches formed delightful patterns on the reflective grids.

At night the web caught the dreams and memories rising from the city. It filled up with Gothic churches, gas stations, liquor stores, functionless buildings rivalling the Watts towers in complexity. At first these were only dimly visible, explained by city scientists as tricks of refraction.

But the day came of their solidity and the people of the city, overcoming their fear, rode the elevators to their City, perched above the abyss on a spider's web.

METAMORPHOSIS NO. 15

A plump mousey-haired girl in a black turtleneck told me this story in my dentist's waiting room.

My boyfriend was a cabalist. He used to tell me about the sexual nature of the universe after we made love. He had this temporary layoff from his job as an injection molder so he bought all these Flair pens in different colors and *reams* of parchment. And he would sit around all day permuting the seventy-two letters of the Names of God. It was real hard to make ends meet on my salary. After a few weeks the Power descended upon him and the letters spilled from his pen. He stopped eating, stopped talking, almost stopped moving. It was easier on the paycheck but not too good in the hominess department if you know what I mean. One day when I was at work the letters began to take on their true forms: vast nebulae, quasars, black holes. And he wrote the True Name. He was consumed by the fire of ecstasy. When I got home most of the stuff was singed, and the stereo was fucked up, and the parchment just ashes. Renter's insurance paid for everything, although I didn't tell them what actually happened.

Sometimes I really miss him.

METAMORPHOSIS NO. 16

Walking on the gray concrete sidewalk of the park, I am caressed by the knotted yarn on my nipples. They rise, looking at the purple storm clouds. My tweed skirt billows in the warm pre-storm air. Ozone and leaves hiss.

Lightning to the left. Every leaf on the maidenhead tree in sharp almost unbearable focus. A sly tree scent blows directly to me. Doors slam and windows close around the park, leaving me alone with the tree. A warm breeze plays between my thighs.

Rain. Small drops, warm, adhering. I'm held by the rain. It soaks the sweater, makes the skirt cling. My breasts begin to run—dissolving gelatinously in the water. Warm pink syrup running over my belly, between my thighs. My pussy snaps at the stream orgasmically. Silver spots boil in front of my eyes.

My chest begins sprouting fine black erectile hairs, a grass in a new spring. A strange fungal growth, a mushroom nourished by the dissolving breasts. I inhale the water, a silkie in the sea, in the strange underwater sea light.

The make-up dissolves from my eyes, my lips. Bones shift with a high keening sound, assuming a new mask. Small hairs sprout on my face. Redbeard.

The swings sing. A young girl, golden hair, sixteen—seventeen. Hot bright-eyed excited by the pounding rain. Her short yellow polka dot summer dress clinging to her thighs. Her breasts summer brown, slapped by the rain.

I rise, my new penis sticking out purple and ugly and hard. She hasn't seen me, but my phallus lifting the hem of the short skirt has seen her. Old One Eye. I pull my skirt off, the rough tweed scratches the head. I run to the swings behind the girl.

Grab her on the swing back. A wet slap of a grab. She squeals. Laughing, she pulls away.

I lunge after her, catching the summer dress. I lead her back. She pulls the dress up, it's her only garment. A lovely blonde patch with pink pouting lips. She backsteps, almost dancing.

Plops down on a patch of flowering plants. A sprout of daisies framed by her wet vagina.

I fall on her, plunging my newfound cock fully into her sweet cleft. Apparently I'm not the first, she bucks against me, her fingers hard on my knotted sweater. I graze on the fine golden down of her neck, plunging deeper and deeper.

Soon it is over. I pull away, she still laughing and babbling. The crushed daisies covered in cum. I pull them out by the roots and toss them over my left shoulder.

I look lovingly at the girl stretched beneath me. I stand, refusing to turn to the noise hissing behind me. I help the girl up, kiss her, send her off with a buttock slap.

I shake myself, the hissing growing louder behind me. The strange anemone between my legs falls. My breasts sprout on my thorax.

I turn. Virginal. Mount the golden-skinned unicorn. Ride away.

METAMORPHOSIS NO. 17

Her nasal overcorrected voice buzzed on and on filling the classroom like flies . . . Ovid, she said, Oh Vid, suggesting a big egg on a pedestal. Wrote in elegiac couplets, she said, looks like a couple of elegies there, those two unshaven men in felt hats. Standing in front of the Egg, separated from it by velvet rope and chrome-plated steel posts.

The man with the congenital blue eyes holds his rimmed hat in wrinkled hands. He is aware of a pink scrotal egg between his balls and rectum. Although encased in his body, internal eyes can see it, a perfect pink oval. The pressure it causes would be explained by his doctor as cancer of the prostate and by his sister who lives with her children in Jersey as womb envy. So he does not tell them. Every day he comes to the warm museum where admission is free and stares at the Egg until his nephew gets off work and takes him home to eat and sleep.

The gray-eyed man, older and more spectral than his companion (most of the city passes him unseeing). He sleeps in the museum in the Egyptology section. Using his cloak of invisibility he passes the guards to the horizontal mummy case. He stands at the Egg, hoping to impregnate it, leaving a mark in this silent universe. Each day through the light interstices of his eyelashes he sees ethereal erectile organs penetrating the great Egg engendering a dragon.

After nine months the blue-eyed man resolves to speak of his burden. Surely the other eggman must be similarly afflicted. After the chamber empties around the two he turns to his companion.

"I've got this terrible pressure."

The gray-eyed man understands that here is a rival father gathering a great shadow-seed. He draws forth a small bronze dagger palmed long ago from the Egyptology room before he learned faith in his invisibility. With a quick flash of motion he

cuts the blue-eyed man from crotch to navel.
A great unfolding. Large green moth wings shake off the blood of the falling man. The phoenix flies out of the chamber. The gray-eyed man leaves the museum.

METAMORPHOSIS NO. 18

She had eschewed birth control as an act of terrorism: she wanted to take a hostage. She hoped to continue the relationship by coercion. A month passed and he did not accede to her demands. There was no media coverage. He left. Two months later the hostage situation ended spontaneously.

She relaxes in the warm bath. The cramps have stopped. The water is a thin red from the blood and greasy from the bath oil. Her thoughts have stopped. Every avenue she'd chosen is now blockaded. There is nowhere to go, therefore she is motionless. She dissolves in the alkahest of the bath water.

Later an unseen hand will open the drain.

METAMORPHOSIS NO. 19

It would be pointlessly macabre and wholly inaccurate to say that the book was bound in human skin and written in blood. It was bound in Moroccan leather and typeset in Garamond (distinguished from the earlier Venetian designs by its horizontal crossbars on the lowercase "e," and by its lighter coloring, and by the graceful ornament of the uppercase letters, particularly in the italic swash initials) on a heavy cream stock. D. B. Bowen sent the book to Miranda Afishce, with thanks for all her

41

advice.

Miranda edited a small magazine. She'd sent D. B. nothing but rejection slips belittling his talent. Maybe he had seen the light. Maybe he was giving up writing to do something useful (such as running a book store).

The book was entitled *A Magical Life: A Work in Regress.* Possibly it was a joke since most of her magazine contained "Extracts from a work in progress"—usually her own. Nevertheless she read it.

And enjoyed it. *A Magical Life* employed the narrative techniques of a complex timeline of delight. The book purported to be the magical diary of the witch Donna Young (1600 – ?) born in Holland and still living in America. It contained numerous accounts of numinous ceremonies, foul perversions, and day-to-day life in the last three centuries.

It had reviews of every book that Donna had read including *A History of Freegate* by Matthew D. Smith III. The *History* was written *backwards.* That is, beginning with the present of the mythical city of Freegate and proceeding toward the past. Successive chapters are written in progressively more archaic language—the last are unreadable iconic codices—similar to Mayan works found on this world. Donna had decided that the *History* was an overlooked classic.

A Magical Life had certain peculiarities. No printing house was listed, there was no copyright date, and the last twenty-five pages were blank.

Two weeks after Miranda read the book, she described it to a friend. She pulled the book from her beautiful mahogany bookcase. The last *forty-seven* pages were blank.

The *Life* now ended with the sentence, "Tomorrow I will visit the Empire State Building." With the new ending everything had changed—the framing and focus were different. During the anxious tea, Miranda could hardly contain her urge to reread it. The friend finally left.

She began a critical article on "Works in Regress." As she wrote, the *Life* shortened again. Again she reread the book.

She called her agent and asked him to cancel her speaking engagements for the next few months. Correspondence began to pile up on her desk. Her magazine's next issue was overdue. The *Life* kept shortening and Miranda continued rereading.

Months later Miranda's agent pulls her from her house. She is completely withdrawn—can't speak or write. She leaves clutching a titleless blank book. Shock treatment may be indicated.

METAMORPHOSIS NO. 20

Boom Times. The air of Minacity is a fine aerosol spray of crude oil, the heartbeats of the pumps, and the dust of yet-to-be-paved streets. Boom Times, and death is the only possible pornography. Every other service can be bought in the shadows of doorways or the tents that sprang up near the depot. Death is the only thrill, the only unexpected spectacle in Minacity.

Quite a crowd gathered when number 23 blew and knocked Jamie Cohen against the back wall of the post office. The oil held her against the yellow-painted wood for a couple of minutes then subsided to a thick gurgle from the well mouth.

Someone cleared her nose and mouth before she drowned in oil. She coughed a little. The vultures left disappointed. Someone carried her to Doc Sadler's office.

It was two months later that she realized she was pregnant. She said the oil well was the father but nobody gave that much credit. There were a lot of unattached births in Minacity. Some folks of a more tender nature allowed as how she was "addled" by the blast, and perhaps the child would resemble his father enough to jog her memory.

She worked in Picken's Grocery up 'til two weeks before the baby was due. She learned to keep the wild talk to herself and the occasional drunken roustabout who wanted to believe that his work in the oilfields unleashed mysterious forces on the earth.

Doc Sadler and Rosa, the madam of the tents, helped her deliver the child. When it first emerged from Jamie they thought it was a black child, which would make for some scandal. But a few contractions proved something different entirely. It was a black sticky mass shaped like a baby—a real life tarbaby. It was soft and boneless—how it survived the birthing without being terribly deformed was a mystery to Doc.

Rosa and Doc held a quiet conference—the same conference that midwives who bring monsters into the world have always held. They decided to smother the child and tell Jamie that it died a few minutes after birth.

They returned to the back room where the resting Jamie and her tarbaby were. And found them gone. Perhaps Jamie had overheard the conference and, moved by motherly love, fled.

Doc saw the tarbaby years later. Doc's practice had become tied to the oil industry, and when the Minacity field played out, he moved on to Houston to the corporate headquarters of the men Minacity had moved into positions of wealth and power. He was given two percent of the company's stock and concerned himself with treating the ailing hearts of high-stress executives.

Once in the corporate building an elevator malfunction took him to a sub-basement. In the brief opening of the doors he saw the tarbaby.

Which of the twenty silent oily golems was Jamie's? What business keeps them swiftly moving in the basement's darkness?

METAMORPHOSIS NO. 21

In front of Grant's Tomb are mosaic benches and arches and walls looking like Poe's undersea city. The bright tiles and flowing forms—introduced by sculptor Padro Pablo Silva in 1972—connect the Tomb through psychic space to the Watts Towers and to ancient fabulous structures whose names men do not know.

It was there that I first saw him. The old man dressed in khaki pants, once white shirt, and grease-caked suspenders. His eyes were the same light blue as the tile shards of his bench. When he spoke—or rather, when he opened his toothless mouth, for no sound issued forth—he would hold his trembling hands in the air as though tracing a cartoon speech balloon.

I was passing by him—I always sought the bench nearest the dead President for my reading—when I saw the cartouches. Cartouches are oval-encased Egyptian hieroglyphics. The oval unifies the symbols into a higher order of meaning. When the old man spoke, a thin cartouche a foot in length and six inches in width formed in the air above him. His hands caught the thin transparent incised plate and laid it on a small clear stack beside his thin legs.

The stack of used words was eight inches tall composed of roughly forty cartouches.

The old man gave me no attention. Fixed upon his task.

That evening I delayed catching my train home to New Jersey. I went to Grant's Tomb but dusk had removed the old man and his deck of see-through sigils.

I left the park and searched book stores in midtown Manhattan. At the fifth book store I found E. A. Budge's translation of the Egyptian *Book of the Dead*. It contains illustrations of the papyrus of Ani with translation into English.

I was able to catch the last train to Jersey.

The next day with phone call and memo I arranged a four-hour lunch. I wanted to see the old man of the tomb, hoping that he was not a fairy, once glimpsed and never again found.

The Moslems believe there are images whose terrifying power is their unforgettability. The Zahir. Once seen they cannot be exorcised from the mind, trapping the mind forever in the past. Like a biology specimen in lucite.

Black children playing basketball. Black adolescents break dancing. Tourists in midwestern clothes and accents.

There he was, just past a tile-covered arch.

He hadn't changed his stale clothes or grown more attentive to his surroundings. Tourists passed us—the transparent cartouches too nearly invisible to attract their attention.

I sat by the old man on the same bench. I grabbed up a few cartouches from his stack. He offered no resistance. I doubt he even noticed.

Their material seems to be a resin plastic cast with little grain. They are cool to the touch and suggestive of carapace. I thumb through the Budge seeking a translation:

"The reader of these glyphs is but a future shadow a dream of the entombed."

The cartouches shatter on the cement. The old man sits alone in hieroglyphic silence.

METAMORPHOSIS NO. 22

Carl Gavitt abandoned TV in favor of his window during the summer months. The window framed a stretch of brownstones and the beginning of a square. When it was open, passing music and conversation would fill his flat with brief bright dopplers.

Carl, a solitary man, would get slowly stoned on Black Russians and watch. There were several mainstays and a cast of extras. The Puerto Rican couple fought constantly in a rapid unknown tongue. The flasher who always appeared on the thirteenth of each month. Two blondes with large breasts and upswept hair rigid with spray. A middle-aged gay with a St. Bernard who eyed the shirtless blacks playing basketball at an improvised hoop hung on the statue's head in the square.

In midsummer about a week after solstice another regular appeared whose eccentric behavior endeared him to Carl above all others. He was a tall Jewish-looking kid with curly hair and intense dark eyes. He would appear near midnight when most folks left the scene. He carried a black bag, a magnifying glass and tweezers. At first Carl thought him a young and overzealous med student.

The kid would stop apparently at random and examine the brownstones, the trees, even parked cars. Occasionally his vigilance would be rewarded and his tweezers would collect a specimen so small as to be invisible to Carl. Then with great care he would transfer it to his bag.

After watching this gathering process for two weeks, Carl purchased a pair of binoculars from a pawn shop near work.

The kid made his nightly round. When he stopped to pluck something from a walnut tree, Carl focused. With painstaking care the kid removed a single strand of spider silk. Carl put down the binoculars, ran downstairs into the street. Enough pedestrian traffic remained for Carl to be inconspicuous. Or so he hoped.

He followed the kid home to a brownstone six blocks distant. Four times the kid stopped to pick a piece of web. At the kid's brownstone Carl waited for a light to indicate the kid's floor or room. When the light came on Carl returned home.

A few days later the kid stopped coming. Curiosity overwhelmed Carl. One day he left work early and went to the kid's apartment.

He knocked. The door was answered by an old lady with fine gray hair carrying knitting needles. She signed that she couldn't speak and motioned Carl in.

Carl didn't see the knitting needle flash into his neck or even feel the venom it injected. He was staring at the old lady's mouth full of cobwebs.

METAMORPHOSIS NO. 23

Sally broke her fingers an hour ago. It changed everything. People always said "you have cool hands." Susan said she could chill champagne with them. Bob loved them unknotting the muscles of his back.

It had been a simple accident, an aberrant invasion of clumsiness into her otherwise graceful life. Laying the two bags of groceries in the seat beside her she pulled the door shut on her left hand, the tips of her three longest fingers. And they broke. They didn't mash or sever or spread. They simply broke.

There was no pain in the breaking. No pain in the sudden loss of movement in the fingers. They were hollow. The interior was white glazed porcelain.

METAMORPHOSIS NO. 24

You make a poor apprentice. If you had read the black letter books I lent you last week you wouldn't have to ask. Yes I know medieval High German is hard—the learning is supposed to be hard, it etches its message in your soul. With the learning and the practice you'll fashion yourself into a proper carved icon for the crowned kings in the hall of the Void. Then you can leave the icon behind and really begin to learn.

Of course I speak in riddles. Three quarters of the Art is concealed in riddles. Old Perdabo used to send his students to the *Alice* books to learn their cabbalah.

Yes, yes, the ritual. Well you helped prepare the incense— you remember gathering the leaves in Central Park last year— told you they'd cook up nice. The spiral path helps my will gather in the whole of the house and protect it from Void demons. Yes, don't look so frightened. Remember the Rule: Fear is failure and the beginning of failure. But you're right about the scratching noise.

Why? You remember Bill. Bill decided he was beyond my lessons and called up Rla TaFla the Lord of Music and Pain in the Void.

Now, now, don't scream. Remember the Rule. Don't make us vulnerable. Yes I know seeing that gray ulcerated frog face at my window is disturbing. Hopefully our barriers will keep it out.

Bill send it against me? No, no, that's what's left of Bill.

METAMORPHOSIS NO. 25

The old coin case was in the back of the store. It was filled with thick copper disks with heavy Doric lettering. They were *oboli*, Professor Strieber recognized them. The Greeks placed the coins in the mouths of their dead that they might pay Charon to ferry them over the Styx into the gray fields of Asphodel in the interior of the Earth. The coins lay in geometric patterns on the dusty blue velvet.

Professor Strieber glances up at the owner's TV. No sound, a black-and-white western. An old woman selling water to the bandits bites a coin to test its metal.

The owner sits in rapt attention. His (her?) formless gray smock reveals little. Strieber begins to call out the proprietor's name but finds he has mislaid it. In fact, he can't quite recall how he came here.

Strieber crosses to the counter intending to ask the price of the coins. The old wooden floor creaks. At the counter he finds that it's not the owner, only a smock draped over an antique chair.

Strieber rings a bell and returns to the coin display. Some finger in his absence has traced a word in the dust: *OPISO*.

Strieber recognizes it for Greek. It means "behind" or "in the future" since the Greeks viewed time as coming up from behind and overtaking one. Thus the past is before one's eyes.

Strieber punches the case. He scarcely has time to place the coin in his mouth before the skeletal hand touches his left shoulder.

METAMORPHOSIS NO. 26

Passing through the SPACE WARP doubles BONUS.
Bumper lights control Entry Gates.
Spelling R-E-N-T-R-Y means Extra Ball.
Hitting moving target on last ball = SPECIAL.

Ozone smell from the old machine. The Kid's fingers real deft, real hot tonight. He's hardly begun to sweat but we all know he's waiting for the Man. You can see it in his eyes, that full moon reflection—he used the lycanthropy drug. Needed it bad tonight.

One of the boys howled as he passed by. Just a joke you know. Kid shot him one of those stares—guy almost pissed on himself in fright. His buddies eased him out of the arcade quick like.

Word passed outside. Place fills up. Everybody watching the Kid see if he can last it out. He's played three games of Space Warp still cool. Got what you call a mineral calm.

Machine's really beginning to spark. Circuitry's old can't take too much this kinda abuse. Getting to be a real musky smell like a wolverine over there.

The Kid's beginning to slip. Pounds on the machine, growls. Wish I could see his eyes.

Feel a nasty wetness on the back of my neck. Sure enough, the Man makes his way through the door. His clothes stale creased with sweat. Makes right for the Kid.

Kid turns. Nothing but the Moon in his eyes—no whites, just

the Moon. Sweat running down his brow, hands clenched like claws. The musk smell is unbearable.

Everybody backs away. The Man puts out his hand. The Kid's trembling so bad he nearly drops the money. A coupla people start to protest the decency of the establishment but the Man just looks through 'em.

The Man throws the Kid against the wall. Rips off his iridescent shirt. He takes a syringe knife from his pocket—runs it along the Kid's shoulder blades, injecting the blue serum as he cuts.

The Kid's skin begins peeling away. Has hair—fur on the inside just like they say. The Kid begins to Change.

The arcade empties.

METAMORPHOSIS NO. 27

The crash is a perfect crystal moment. The afternoon sun golden like weak tea softened the air, making it a better medium. The boy in the blue car has a lovely scream, tape recordings of his scream will be hawked to vampires through various underground markets for years. The blood of the couple in the red Mustang gives a high keening—as spilt blood always does—calling to spirits in hidden places throughout the City.

Anemones and hyacinths, bright red and blood violet, sprout from the asphalt. Such flowers live on the keening of the blood—slowing the vibrations to a quiet echo of vegetation.

The City flower sellers, old women with faded wooden pushcarts, come to gather the flowers for lovers' bouquets.

A dark man walks from the garbage-strewn alley. The flower ladies part for him. He opens the crushed door of the Mustang, pulls the girl's bloody body out.

With the ease of practice he slings the body over his shoulder. He closes the door, returns to his alley. The flower ladies finish their task and depart as sirens arrive.

He walks down the alley between tan dumpsters to a hidden door. He carries his burden inside to a hall lit with the gas lamps of another era. A dirty adolescent boy runs to him. Words and a few dollars are exchanged and the boy heads downtown.

The man walks down the hall past a massive oaken door. He dumps the body on a cloth covered table. He undresses her.

He lifts the nude body. By now he is also covered in the clotting blood. He heaves the body into a boiling cauldron. He goes to clean himself. An hour later he returns, lifts the clean skeleton with tongs to the table. He begins to wrap a flesh-covered sheet around it.

The boy bursts in with a single hyacinth in his hand. He touches the flower to the lips of the now perfect body.

She rises from the table.

METAMORPHOSIS NO. 28

Myrna is a good mother. She stands at the third floor window of her brownstone in the fashionable fifties. Myrna watches a young black woman raped on her stoop. Myrna closes the heavy green curtains, goes to the children's playroom. Such good children, so small.

She brings them cookies. She brings them low-fat high-protein vitamin D-enriched milk. She's sure they're all heterosexual. She gives them educational durable nontoxic toys.

Myrna switches on the TV. The news reports that a Puerto Rican boy was caught in the closing door of an IRT local at Columbus Circle. The boy's head struck each concrete support of the tunnel. He stopped screaming after the third collision. At the next station the doors opened automatically, dropping what was left of him on the extended grill. Thirty people in the car.

No one had pulled the emergency brake cord, bright red, labeled in two languages.

She puts the children to bed. They will have sweet dreams. She goes to the courtyard behind the brownstone.

Myrna pulls off her jeans. Myrna pulls off her panties. She opens her vagina to the fullest. She goes to the corner of the brownstone. She spreads her cuntlips over the smog-blackened stone. It's painful at first, with so much to absorb. The doors and windows are easier, being smooth. It takes four hours to completely encase the brownstone.

Ponderously, Myrna makes her way out of the City. She is a good mother.

METAMORPHOSIS NO. 29

All of us are fascinated by the future, because that is where we will live the rest of our lives.

—The Amazing Criswell
prologue to *Plan 9 from Outer Space*

High school biology teaches us that each organism is a self-contained system run by a vastly efficient string of DNA. Professional biology has largely discarded this paradigm (at least on the cellular level). Beginning with such obvious cases of interdependence as lichens, study progressed to protozoan and coelenterate systems (sea anemones), where "this symbiotic process has become even more intimate and the photosynthesizing plant components have degenerated into mere particles within the cell closely resembling the chloroplasts which give green plants their pigmentation." [From "What is a Micro-Organism?" M. R. Pollock, *New Scientist*, 27:637-639, 1965.]

Pollock points out that many of the organelles (such as

mitochondria) possess a particular DNA of their own. Such minute structural features have some degree of self-reproductive autonomy—pointing to independent evolutionary origin. Some bacteria and protozoa joined the team early and stayed on unconcerned with outer evolutionary changes in their hosts. Pollock also points out that there are recognizable extrachromosomal activities in bacteria, such as drug resistance.

Modern biology experimentally introduced extraneous genetic material into rats as long ago as 1964. Mouse chromosomes and man chromosomes will multiply happily side-by-side.

What is not generally known is that the process of incorporating living entities into cells will have a macrosystems counterpart (soon to be seen in our larger cities with a cast of thousands). Soon entire organisms will be incorporated. Mrs. Nicholl's poodles will merge with her body—their tiny yapping heads taking the place of her breasts. Slum dwellers will develop carapaces as a result of a new intimate cockroach symbiosis. Minotaurs will fight one another in Spanish bullrings.

One of the best ways to destroy your faith in evolution is to read Darwin's *Origin of the Species*. Darwin proposed "survival of the fittest" where "fittest" is defined in terms of survival. His theory is based on differential reproduction. Differential reproduction means that some species multiply by leaving more offspring than one-for-one, while others leave one-for-one and remain stable, and others leave fewer than one-for-one. Why does this happen? Darwin's answer is: because some multiply, others remain stable, dwindle, or die out. Darwin gets away with a tautology. I am by no means the only individual to notice this. See *Darwin Revisited* by Norman MacBeth (1971), pages 47-8; Waddington (1957); Coffin as cited in Scriven (1959); Birch and Ehlrich (1967); and

Peters (1976).

All of these scholars are upset that Darwin's evolution is a tautology not a theory, and therefore cannot be empirically tested.

I see no reason why evolution shouldn't be a tautology. In a vast system, which is regarded as being without entelechy (i.e., no one is driving the bus), any description would have to contain tautological elements. It happened, it happened this way.

On the other hand, fictional systems can be presumed to have entelechy. There is an inner purpose—if we concede that the authors are part of a fictional system.

Unfortunately, the strong internal rules of *Uncle Ovid's Exercise Book* have mutated the bus driver into an amoeba whose pseudopods cannot reach the steering wheel.

METAMORPHOSIS NO. 30

Tomas died almost instantaneously in the crash. He finds himself floating in the silvery morning air two meters above the flaming Cessna. The frost-covered grass circles to wet grass then to burning grass. The smoke and the steam drift through Tomas.

A gull flies far overhead carrying a streamer of paper in its beak like an Angelus in an old woodcut. The bird releases its cream-colored streamer. Tomas floats upward to catch it, the sound of his former flesh popping in the oily fire having no appeal. He snatches the paper. It is roughly twice the size of a fortune cookie slip. Tomas had thought it larger. No, it's Tomas who has expanded, he's like a Macy's balloon. He doesn't like the sunlight shining through him—he pulls himself together.

Ah, that's better.

The paper's now six feet long. It has a black letter inscription:

Oh! Nobly born, let not thy mind be distracted!

Hm. That's familiar. Beginning of the *Bardo*, the Tibetan Book of the Dead. The other side has a computergraphic inscription:

In case of actual emergency you would have been instructed where to tune.

The paper becomes intangible and drifts through Tomas's fingers.

An almost transparent larva, shaped like a thistle with rotten tentacles, sucks the paper in. The larva drifts toward Tomas. Tomas decides to leave.

When he tries to move, the landscape blurs around him. A new scene vibrates into focus.

A dark brick building. A many-storied rectangle with two lesser storied wings extending the sides of the rectangle opposite Tomas. The vertex of the rectangle toward Tomas is frustrated at ground level by a set of heavy glass doors over which bunting hangs:

WELCOME TOMAS

Tomas descends to ground level. Passes through the doors—not by opening them but by a new complicated action now native to him.

A vast corridor of gray linoleum. He drifts along. Past more doors, these white-painted wood with brass push panels instead of knobs. Inside is an operating room. An enormously fat man on the table with a great opening cut into his chest.

The P.A. system activates with a staticky bark:

—Oh! Nobly born, let not thy mind—

—Switch that off, nurse.

Until he spoke, the grizzly surgeon and the green-smocked nurse had been invisible. Now they came into unbearably sharp focus. Their faces didn't behave properly—as Tomas watches, older and younger masks appear on them. The nurse switches off a cream toggle. The surgeon looks at Tomas.

—Now, there, nothing to worry about. Nothing like a coupla hundredweight of flesh to make a good, fatty prison for the soul. The surgeon grabs something in Tomas' chest. Everything reels out of focus.

METAMORPHOSIS NO. 31

I knew D. before he began writing the *Changes*. He got hung up on the short-short form, the condensed experience (coex! coex!) or what I called the Campbell's Soup school of fine LitRature. Here's an example of one of the stories:

AND A RUBBER BAND MOTOR

Following Lautreamont's dictum that all should make poetry we all made some. With an X-acto knife and some airplane glue and a propeller from a promotional toy found in a box of Cocoa Puffs we fashioned an airplane from the raw poesy. Spun it full of potential energy and flew it out the back window. It arced up against a white painted beam—the skeleton for the never-to-be-built patio roof—and shattered. The pieces fell all over Father, interrupting his dream of Terri Garr. He stormed inside and walloped us kids good. We learned not to make poetry with grown-ups around.

It's a pretty typical story. It's got the short sentences, misses out on a lot of images: the daylilies in the long rectangular bed by the cement patio or the black bricks of the house. It ends with the artistic self-justification. (I suspect him to be a little paranoid after his speed freak days.)

Living one apartment door away, I became his constant companion, having lotsa unwanted free time due to a January

Don Webb

layoff. Morning tea around eleven . . .

Sure, I was there the last day. D. hadn't said anything in a while (but what's new?). I looked over my Red Zinger at him. His mouth was forming a word but no sound came out and his brow was covered in sweat. I guess he'd stumbled upon the ultimate condensation.

There was a *pop!* and he imploded—like on old-style TV picture contracting to the last dot. A little black dot surrounded by little blue pictures—the Rice campus during a flood . . . a marriage in New Orleans . . . losing a brown mackintosh during a Lubbock wind storm . . .

The gravitation got most of the furniture. It got most of my past so I live in his.

METAMORPHOSIS NO. 32

The seventh year of an unhappy marriage. Anne parades a new green dress, apparently solid sequins. Arthur looks as though he can feel the hempen rope slip around his neck. Why was it always like this?

—Anne, how could you?

—But it's such a pretty thing and I spend so little on myself.

—What did you buy it on?

—Our Visa card.

—No way we can pay for it when the bill comes.

—Well, it's not my fault that you can't make enough money.

Arthur pauses, any speech or action smothered by ear-pounding rage. Why was their life like this? Arthur glances out the window and for the first time he sees the man holding the cue cards.

METAMORPHOSIS NO. 33

dead cat passed around for fucking by a group of adolescent boys until it got too ripe when only Charlie would fuck it earning him the tasty nickname of Maggot Dick. Seventeen years a successful law practice a BMW and his blood brothers would begin telephone calls with "Hey, Maggot." Seventeen years being well past the statute of limitations Charles decided to end the practice.

To this end Charles stole a rare copy of *Almadel* from his alma mater's world-famous rare book collection. Charles was an excellent student.

Charles got a Polaroid of his gang and carefully cut his own image from the picture. He placed it in a square lettered with degenerate Hebrew letters and European corruptions of the Name—why do you think they're called spells anyway?

He burned black roses and sulfur for a month in adoration to Beelzebub Lord of the Flies. And each night at midnight a tiny automatic projector would play the matter transmitter scene from *The Fly*, an old Vincent Price movie where the hero develops a fly's head and claw. Charles waited for his friends to change.

Poor Charlie, he underestimated the magic of naming. After seventeen years of being called Maggot Dick, he was like a lightning rod to the spell's electricity.

His wife killed him two days afterward with a can of Raid.

METAMORPHOSIS NO. 34

There are many Chinese elms in Amarillo, Texas. The Chinese elm is a sturdy breed. Its quick growth and resistance to blight (Dutch elm disease) and drought have endeared the breed to

Don Webb

landscapers. In the spring of 1999 several quarter-sized green buds appeared on Chinese elm branches. The normal bud is the size and shape of a raindrop on waxed paper, and has a brown carapace.

The *Amarillo Globe-News* produced color pictures of these wondrous buds. Experts from as far away as Texas A&M were consulted. Many theories were advanced; most dealt with long-term radiation leaks from the Pantex plant. In mid-March the buds bloomed. Their flowers were small pastel ovoids which glowed at night. In short, Chinese lanterns.

The gentle light transformed neighborhoods. Despite the low temperatures, outdoor mah-jongg parties became fashionable. Cloth World held a special sale on pongee.

The "Newspaper Bible" in the *Amarillo News-Globe* began reprinting the *Tao-te-Ching* on April 1, 1999. On April 7, a *ki-rin*, the fat blue Chinese unicorn, appeared on Georgia Street. On April 14 the phoenix landed on the Westgate Mall parking lot. The giant tortoise walked down Polk Street on April 21.

On the 28th, the celestial dragon, Tien-Lung, appeared majestically from the clouds. His silver-and-blue body contrasted fantastically with the West Texas sunset. He circled the city thrice and then exhaled a fine rose-colored mist. The mist transported Amarillo to an East that never was.

The future is to be dissolved and mixed very dilutely (in accordance with strictest homeopathic principles) with the present. He who does nothing *(wu-wei)* can move heaven and earth.

METAMORPHOSIS NO. 35

For seventeen years, Paul Ackner commuted to the City. The 7:30 train brought him to McInner Station, three blocks west seven blocks north and another half block west from his office.

The reverse process and the 5:15 train took him home to Julia, the station wagon, and the how-did-your-day-go.

Paul distilled the perfect film from this. At McInner he would see the graying portly executive nod, smile. On the corner of Dulwith and Peoria, while he waited for the walk light, three overly made-up secretaries would cross in a perpendicular fashion. He would engage in a sexual fantasy concerning the redhead who walked point for the female triangle. End sexual fantasy as three nuns walking south on Peoria came into view.

The film replayed every day. Occasionally one or more of the actors would be absent. Only the gaps were noticed, providing new scripts: where's Red today? only two nuns?

Over the years, bit actors took color roles. On Soleri Avenue (half block west) summer provided the flower man, whose first appearance every year created a shock of orange gladiolas as a "surprise" for Julia. Christmas time was marked by the Salvation Army Santa Claus collecting a toll as the three coated secretaries passed.

One Tuesday Paul's boss came to him and said a new data processing system would be installed in the office next Sunday and could he come down to supervise?

The 7:30 train didn't run on weekends. But since the crew wasn't to arrive until 9:30 anyway, the 8:15 would suffice.

The suburban station lacked its business-suited hum. Paul was one of only three passengers. In the tradition of territorialism, each rode in a different car.

At McInner Paul detrained alone. The three blocks west were equally silent. At the Peoria and Dulwith intersection he began his sexual fantasy about Red although she was not there to provide visual stimulus.

Immersed in his fantasy he walked the seven blocks north. At the corner of Peoria and Soleri Avenue was a tower. A windowless tower covered in a malachite mosaic and topped with an onion dome.

Paul stared at the tower for a long time. There was no Soleri Avenue in sight. He didn't come to Soleri Avenue on Sunday so

Don Webb

why did he suppose Peoria Street did?

Paul drops his briefcase full of notes on the new data processing system and interface. He begins to climb the tower, the rough mosaic affording adequate finger and shoe holds. Three-quarters of the way up Paul rigidly freezes. Cracks appear in his skin, his suit and his shoes.

The cicada emerges—larval no longer. Soon its wings will carry it away.

METAMORPHOSIS NO. 36

It is advisable for those who wish to travel to Carraleur to do so in groups because of the fetish towers. The brass fetish towers cluster around all the passes to the mountainous land of Carraleur. When a group passes such a tower, a strange madness will seize one of its number. He or she will develop a fixed stare of terror. Despite his or her companions' cries, the afflicted will run to a tower and begin to climb.

Often the group will try to restrain the mad one, but his madness gives great strength. Bonds are broken, holds are cast off, obstacles are kicked away. The stricken one clambers up, finding easy footing in the rough green surface. Once he is upon the tower, group members become afraid to claim their companion. They watch the climb to the very top. At the summit the mad one gives agonizing screams. His body turns to brass. It is not a quick metamorphosis—the process requires three to four minutes.

Only then does the party see that the tower is composed of twisted human forms. Only then are they free to proceed down the path to Carraleur. The expression of the victim may not be one of pain, but perhaps one of ecstasy. It is said that the land of Carraleur is one of Unending Delight. Certainly no one returns who travels there.

In my old age I may risk the journey, but for now I am content in my small cottage. With my spyglass, I can barely see the towers.

METAMORPHOSIS NO. 37

I hear you call for help on my answering machine. I leave for the airport immediately. I haven't been here in years—it's much larger than I remember. I park the car in long-term parking and make the long trek to the terminal. The noise inside deafens me. Loudspeakers buzz out cryptic but important sounding messages. I pause just inside the door, my back to a pebble-inlaid concrete column. I see the ticket counter of the airline you told me to take. Perhaps I should've called you first—told you that help was on its way.

The line at the counter is slow, but we are protected from the crush of people by comforting red velvet ropes. The dark Indian man in front of me seems relaxed—he's no doubt used to crowds. Eventually my time comes up. I have to shout and repeat and shout again. Finally the girl at the counter hands me a terribly flimsy looking piece of paper. My chance of actually making the flight is based on this slip. She gestures vaguely in the direction of the gate. I leave the safe area.

If a bar of gold touches a bar of steel even for a moment, some of the gold molecules leap across to join the steel and some of the steel to replace the gold. It's a scientific fact.

My gate is on the other side of the airport. I shall have to cross the long lobby and negotiate two long corridors before I arrive. The prospect makes me giddy. I am jostled from behind by someone leaving the safe area anxious to seek their gate.

I plunge blindly forward, fighting my way through the crowd. Their faces are terrible Japanese ghost masks. Each of them shoves, jostles, obstructs, intent on foiling my straight

63

Don Webb

line of travel. Their contact is rough and unending. My molecules are being spread thin. I am being worn away—replaced molecule by molecule like a petrified log.

By the time I reach the gate, "I" shall be gone entirely. I will be completely replaced. Someone else will arrive to help you. Someone we don't know.

METAMORPHOSIS NO. 38

The old man has sea-green kitten eyes. His face frozen. He is an insect addict. Every day he injects massive doses of royal jelly through long, long needles past his tear duct directly into his pineal gland. Slowly chitin replaces infirm flesh, eyes facet. Soon his metamorphosis will be complete. Small feelers will grow from his face for direct connection to the memory core. Useless parts will fall away. And as an insect, he will mimic a cluster of printed cards.

Then his software will click and slither through the machine. Programmers on the night shift hearing the shrill insect music. White lab coats making slapping motions at the backs of their necks. Too late, their pudgy faces fall forward, dead noses pressing against the green light of the cathode ray tube.

A million larvae twisting in their brains. They escape as fly-ash from the incinerator, small crystalline patterns airborne, settling in diode bridges, micro-flipflops. Even under the big red button. Numbers will spill out. Virus noise riding through the grid everywhere. Numbers from the old man's DNA.

The old man smiles in his enchanted loom.

METAMORPHOSIS NO. 39

In lustrations, third of first texts hieroglyphic—would the English like "serious" while level? You call us Silence Group. So be it. In silence we move. Great primary shadow bodies, all shadows are linked together. A dissection on the march—when we march, our footsteps echo around the planet. Hear the silent slithering of the shadows?

In the mist itself, encounters involving dauntless Big Time transcripts. No omniscient author. We can stick you in a portable hole and forget about you. I'll check my shooting, out those forces roll. Son, traveller and possession, titled form. Female which builds extraordinary—a couple of true pictures from the scrapbook culminating in animated readings with permutated recordings and projections throughout.

The scrapbook itself being magical, it was labeled Book of Toth. Twenty-two pictures, making for an incredible number of permutations. Set suggested we take the paper cutter and cut each card in quarters. Then, matching four quarters at random, broadcast the picture subliminally during *I Love Lucy* reruns. Need new archetypes, he sez. We protested, of course. Sacred motto: "Hieroglyphic Silence." But Set, no doubt remembering his Black Panther days, threatened to tear Osiris' bones apart and throw them to Typhon. So we relented, what with Isis on the necrophilia charge and not being allowed in to see a Clint Eastwood film.

We gave him the group's scrapbook. Record of our best tour ever. Toth was fit to be hog-tied, so we hog-tied the ibis-headed sucker.

Then the ape of Toth broke into the studio, gibbering in unknown tongues, making straight for the green-painted paper cutter (Set stole it from a nearby elementary school).

They wrestled. Set was really pissed. He caught the ape's arm and sliced off the right hand with the paper cutter. Snicker-snack!

65

With great howls and splashing of blood, the ape fled the studio. Set wiped the paper cutter off with some stiff brown paper towels (also stolen from the elementary school). He shuffled the pictures, stiff with construction paper backs. Toth had glued 'em all with Krazy Glue. Set pulled the first three for the experiment. One was Bast, filling jugs of well water before we crossed the Mojave. Toth had labeled it Tzaddi—the star. The second was a polaroid of Osiris sitting in his lazy boy at home, regal in his russet-and-olive suit. Toth labeled it The Emperor.

The third was a black-and-white snapshot of Set himself with some groupies. They were chained up, strictly an S&M scene. Toth, not being real keen on the subject, had written the Devil.

Set took all three cards, shuffled and cut them. One cut longwise and one cut shortwise.

He pulled four quarters from the pile and began to paste them into the new scrapbook. Big Time Transcripts. Upper right Set, upper left Osiris, lower right Osiris, lower left Set. Legend read "The Empevil."

The cut project was a disastrous success. Next year father-produced child abuse rose fifty percent.

The Tour was great. When we march our footsteps echo around the world.

METAMORPHOSIS NO. 40

Being the supplier for the President ain't easy. If the press ever catches you—it would have been better that your mother had not borne you. Getting frisked by Secret Service men, automata of Puritan hyper-morality, is no joke. Those boys check seven inches up.

To avoid detection, a variety of ruses are employed. The

successful supplier must always break his routines. Erase his personal history and tangle others' world-lines. Sometimes I'm the White House linen service man. Sometimes a turbaned ambassador from an oil-rich emirate. Sometimes male. Sometimes female.

When the Pres comes down with paranoia, even more elaborate methods of contact must be devised. I've flown in on UFO's.

I've tunneled in from beneath, past the laser grid. Dodging the animated skeletons in the sub-basement, an eerie reminder of Warren G. Harding's voodoo. And finally up to the Oval Office, riding in a dumbwaiter.

Lately the Big Man's been on a natural kick. Fresh cactus. Yage vines cut days ago.

The big favorite is mandrake. Roots cleaned and washed for Presidential munching.

I was traveling through the forest, a dark deep glade growing over a landfill at the headwaters of the Potomac. I had a big black dog. You pull the mandrake from the ground—the scream of the root kills the hound. You can tell the potency of the root by the volume of the scream. The dog's body I sell to a taco place—no questions asked.

Anyway, I'm in the woods and been looking for mandrake for about two hours. The pollution beginning to clear and I can see the stars.

I come upon a granite pillar. At first I make it for a tombstone, but a tombstone wouldn't be here on the site of an ancient landfill. I flashlight it to read the inscription.

Three parallel inscriptions (shades of Rosetta). Latin, English, and (maybe) Iroquois. English one says:

I ERECT THIS PILLAR TO THE

GREAT GOD NODENS

ON ACCOUNT OF THE MARRIAGE I SEE

UNDER THE SHADE.

The dog whimpers and backs away. Straight from a B movie. In the shade of the pillar some mushrooms grow. Golden yellow caps, white gills, about seven inches tall. *Pantheria amatia*. Deadly fly agaric. Panthers of the night of the Gods.

I kick the dog, releasing it in the forested night. I chose two of the larger caps for my Ziploc bag. I'll have muscimole-bearing fruit for the Pres tomorrow.

Dressed as a Texan tourist I visit the White House. Dart into a john after passing the Lincoln bedroom. Into the blue-tiled stall.

I flush three times and the wall slides open. Two Secret Service goons grab me. The search begins quietly, the only noise being clothes pulled off my body. The mushrooms are in my Stetson.

After being probed, poked, and frisked, the goons usher me into a secret conference room.

I smile, pull the plastic-wrapped fungus out of my hat. Toss it on the long table.

"Muscarine, sir." The President raises one eyebrow in imitation of Leonard Nimoy.

He pulls the bag apart with long yellowed fingernails. The mushrooms make their way into his mouth in little white bits. Clotted cream.

Five minutes pass after he consumes the shrooms. His eyes dilate. A smile warms his features. He sez, "Lust huge polished reporters! Steel. Bring the wife deviant. We home deviant video drain." Spittle collects at the end of his Presidential chin. I guess the stuff is coming on pretty hard.

"Are you all right, sir?"

"Armadillos in every pot."

His flesh begins to run. Metamorphosis has set in. His hands become great claws; his head degenerates into ropy tentacles. His back sprouts large chitinous wings. With a quick scuttle, he throws open the window. He sails out on Washington thermals into the night sky over Capitol Hill. I'd better be going. 'Bye now!

METAMORPHOSIS NO. 41

The doorknob opens a blue eye. Check. No one's at home. The hinges eject their bolts in rapid fire. One. Two. Three. The doorknob turns, freeing the locking bolt. The door pivots clockwise, outward forty-five degrees. The outer doorknob opens its sulfur-yellow eye. The door stands on the porch of the suburban brick split-level. It is midmorning—the neighborhood is quiet. The lock sniffs the air. It can detect its goal, far away and faint. The door pivots on one corner and then another until it reaches the edge of the concrete porch. It braces itself then falls onto the St. Augustine grass. It rights itself and continues on.

It waddles as fast as a tired jogger. It pants softly. Neighborhood dogs bark and howl at the wooden intruder. It proceeds down the sidewalk for three blocks, finds a through street and turns left. Six more blocks to the freeway. Once there it makes its way along the weedy glass-strewn right-of-way. Some of the motorists see it in their mad plunge, but the pressure of the traffic prevents them from stopping to investigate.

Ed Blum, hitchhiker and philosopher, spots the door approaching. He lowers his thumb and runs in terror. But Ed Blum isn't the door's goal.

Half a mile further on is a deserted house. Gaps for door and windows. Little roof. It was deserted nine years ago on this day—the ninth day of the ninth month. The three nines give it a special structure. These coordinates have long been awaited.

The door comes to the house. It inserts itself in the door frame. It closes its eyes and grows new hinge pins. Nine days after its insertion the door opens. Not connecting the inside of the house with the outside—in fact from outside it appears to have vanished. It has opened in the Mirror World.

Aeons ago people could pass through mirrors as easily as Alice. There they learned strange and wonderful magics. Those people living in the Mirror World waged terrible war on those who lived in our world. The magicians of this world were able to work a terrible curse on the mirror denizens. The mirror people were forced to mimic everything they saw. Passage between the worlds stopped and mirrors became cold and glassy.

The mirror people have not forgotten their terrible defeat. They have waited to escape into our world and wreak their vengeance. They are leaving their world and entering the deserted house one by one. Violence increases daily but no one knows its source.

When next you look in a mirror, watch carefully. As you turn away the mirror man smiles a secret smile.

METAMORPHOSIS NO. 42

Dae Ulmob caresses the faded tattoos that brought him to the city of Sibs. Disgusting old man, his teeth rotten with age, he sits alone at the cafe. Began his career as an "elaborate ideogram boy" an illiterate runner whose message is tattooed by the scribes. Five times he made the run across the desert, ending here in Sibs with no unmarked skin.

Most of the "elaborate ideogram boys" die of a painful skin cancer, thus relieving the scribes of their upkeep. Dae Ulmob continues to live and fester—becoming an outcast.

Of late Dae has frequented the cafe on the Rock, an extrusive basaltic reminder of the city's fiery past. Dae alone feels a hum from the Rock. And as he sits at his table it crawls up his feet and through his bones. Dae believes that slowly a message is being etched on his bones—a message from the Rock to the City.

He has tried to tell the others, but hampered by his barbaric Northern accent and near toothless mouth. . .

Dae drinks the sweet tea at the cafe, his only luxury. The

owners would like him to leave—to wander into the red desert and die. But he is the property of the scribes and his withered tattooed person is sacrosanct.

Each day, as the vultures go to feed in the alabaster towers, Dae feels the Rock. Soon. It'll be soon.

Dae caresses his flesh. With a sharp motion he knocks over his cup, scattering tea on the stone floor. It is done. The message has been received.

Dae flings out his arms. His bones burst forth at his fingertips. They are red branches growing rapidly.

Within days Lemuria sinks under the weight of the coral.

METAMORPHOSIS NO. 43

Now Mr. Williams was an owner and by his owning owned more and more and eventually owned a whole section of the City. Now Mr. Williams didn't live in his section nor was it named after him—in fact it was named after the race of most of its inhabitants. Mr. Williams never visits his section 'cause he's scared of the folk and building inspectors never visit it 'cause they're scared of Mr. Williams.

One day in the tiny rusty mailboxes a little notice printed in twenty point caps on cheap pink paper appeared. It read:

NOTICE OF EVICTION

and it gave a date. It didn't mention the highway or how the land to border the highway-to-be was too valuable for them to live their lives on it. Nor did it mention the money from actual and potential deals that would give Mr. Williams the escape velocity to join the high orbit ranks of the very rich.

But these things were read between the lines 'cause when you read the victor's language you gotta read all the hidden information as well as the iceberg tip. After all "our sea" is a victor's name.

So a meeting was called. And a hat passed around. And a visit made to a grimy little shop in Mr. Williams' section called Burroughs, Blackstone, Crow, and Dee, Psychic Agents.

Mr. Williams' mailbox, which was in a post office and filtered by three levels of secretaries, received a note engraved on Egyptian papyrus which read: "All is forgiven. You are cordially invited to the Last Block Party of Nineteenth Street next Friday evening at 8:30. We think you are a Big Man."

Mr. Williams, afraid of the notice and of the party and of his tenants, is more afraid of being laughed at and bad press and injunctions. So he goes to the party. He drives his own car, giving his chauffeur the night off and hoping to God not to see him there.

Mr. Williams walks up to the streamers and lights and party sounds. There's banners and bunting and long tables with food and drink, but no people. The party sounds come from speakers—on poles stuck through broken windows, ghetto blasters laying on the sidewalk and cheap car woofers sticking out of gutter drains.

Mr. Williams takes all this for a set-up. Every window and doorway and shadow become so many eyes, teeth, guns. Figuring he's surrounded, he decides to enjoy his last meal.

He goes to the punch bowl and fills a cheap plastic champagne glass. The punch is a red fruit juice and a cheap smoky bourbon in apparently equal quantities. Halfway through his second glass he begins to notice how low the doorways are. How small the parked cars. The table only comes to his knees. Mr. Williams, we think you are a Big Man.

The party noises shut off and are replaced by a hot jazz piece. Loud with Miles Davis' trumpet, Larry Young's electric piano, Jack DeJohnette's drums and many others, jamming freely. The music's very loud and Mr. Williams doesn't like it. Small men run from the doorways. Pygmies.

Mr. Williams runs. Stepping over buildings, electric cables

snapping on his knees. He runs fast but they are always behind him, growing smaller and smaller. He trips over a concrete barrier—the overpass of the traffic loop surrounding the city.

The giant's body lands in the field with a loud crash. It begins to stiffen because of the poison. Thick bricks form out of the skin. Windows from the pores, wiring from nerves, air conditioning from lungs. The people move in the next day.

METAMORPHOSIS NO. 44

It was the annual exotic vacation of the Association of Nigger-Killing Sheriffs. They were sand-sailing the Australian outback in a desert skiff, the H.M.S. *Pequod.* . The sheriffs took turns harpooning abos and pulling them behind in the silicon wake.

The skiff was three days out when it docked at Victoria Island. The sheriffs ran around drinking Foster wearing black Stetsons comparing notches in their .45s.

Another skiff moored at the island. An archaeological expedition from great cyclopean ruins where they were following a Miskatonic expedition way back from before the Big War. They were carrying strange metal lockers engraved in curvilinear characters of a bygone race. Shadowed whispers around the bar of great rugose cones with four long tentacles.

The sheriffs sail the next day heading for the dig—"I always wanted to see me some ru-ins." Two days of sailing and only one abo running the whole trip. Mr. McPhearson bagged him with the aft harpoon. The abo got off a boomerang shot which sizzled nicely against the skiff's forcefield. Everybody toasted McPhearson—"Not a finer sheriff in the country"—with bourbon and branch water.

The lawmen weighed anchor within a city block of the ruins. They broke out torches and descended into the great masonry

73

halls bent at crazy angles after eons of geologic strain.

In the lowest levels great iron doors, strongly barred, were marked with the footprints of an invisible being. Five circles in a star. Eerie whistling sound.

"Well, how we gonna shoot it?"

And the sheriffs talked, black Stetsons bobbing in the electric torchlight. As they spoke, Bensi-who-carries-his-head-in-his-hands, God of Whistling Winds, appeared among them.

On moonlit nights among the ancient halls of the Great Race one can hear the echoes of the American south. Sometimes a black Stetson flies in the whistling wind.

METAMORPHOSIS NO. 45

A

William Burroughs theorized, "Language is a virus from outer space." Critics fixed on this as an example of failed s-f in Burroughs' work. Critics were overlooking the studies of P. W. Hodge, R. S. Rajan, and D. Tomandle on micrometeor debris (mainly commentary). Reasoning from the similarity of certain structures in the debris to Type I carbonaceous chondrites, Sir Fred Hoyle and Chandra Wickramasinghe deduce that the quasi-chondrites might be viral particles. Their views may be found in *New Scientist* 76:402-404, 1977. Viruses from outer space may well account for outbreaks of heretofore unrecognized epidemic diseases. Hoyle and Wickramasinghe cite the abrupt appearance of references to particular diseases. The common cold appears in the literature in the 15th century.

In addition to epidemiological effects, viruses cause mutations by adding genes to existing DNA. The viral matter may lengthen the self-concatenating strings of life and solve evolutionary conundrums unexplainable by Darwinian (or

Gouldian) models (vide *New Scientist* 77:139, 1978).
William Burroughs was wrong in one particular. They are
not words from outer space. They are punctuation.

B

the shape of loneliness in a warning

C

Mike Trampier was struck by a period (from outer space) on
his way to work. He felt nothing. It lodged in a pore on his
forehead and began burrowing inward. By coffee break it had
broken into a mucus-producing cell of his nose and was
rewriting genetic code. At the end of the day Mike was an inch
and a half shorter. No one noticed save for Mike. He thought
he'd stretched his shirt.

In the evening he took his girl to see Akira Kurosawa's *Ran*.
Nearly twenty percent of Mike's cells were turning out periods.
He itched like crazy. He went to the restroom for a good scratch.
In the mirror he saw that he'd become ink black. The sudden
surge of adrenaline kicked all his ADP boosters. The viral DNA
multiplied like crazy. Before he could run out of the john he was
three foot eight inches tall. His clothes fell off. Realizing he
needed professional help, Mike ran out of the theater.

Sally Otus, who runs the candy counter, remembers seeing
a small black boy—very fat—running out. It's four blocks from
the Village Four Cinema to the hospital.

Two blocks later Mike became perfectly spherical. His
diameter was six inches and rapidly dwindling. He rolled off
the sidewalk and bounced into the gutter

     . . . .   .

       .   .

      . .   .   .

He became a full stop on a browned elm leaf. Summer rains
washed him away

METAMORPHOSIS NO. 46

A small—roughly man-shaped—piece of ground, where they burned the wino last year and stood in a circle listening to him scream, in strange colors surrounded by a circle of ash trees and hopelessness. No grass or weeds grew there next year, and the snow was uncommon quick to melt from the spot as though it held heat from the holocaust. Those who had witnessed the burning as circus had disappeared with the coming of winter, leaving only the cold echo of motorbikes.

The spot became a legacy to high school dimestore Satanists who gathered to drink beer and tell unlikely horrific lies. On Beltane they boldly sacrificed a helpless Siamese cat, cutting its white throat and darkening the ground. Crudely done and incorrectly incanted, the ceremony attracted Attention from the nether regions. A particular vibration, a certain electricity of air, was breathed upon the place. An unhealthy fog marked by chill upon the back and the constriction of glands.

In mid-May a tender green shoot appeared in the center of the spot. It grew rapidly into a small grassy plant dominated by a single vegetal spire. In August the spire bloomed into a single bell-like flower almost black in its darkness.

Its smell, sweet and cloying, penetrated into the whole of the little town. Because of its sweetness the town's inhabitants began moving slowly with dreamy smiles. Life softened, quieted.

In September the flower began to die and the city of mirages shifted in the autumn light and faded away.

METAMORPHOSIS NO. 47

It's been a bad summer for locusts (or rather a good summer for locusts and a bad summer for everyone else). Usually the only stain on the garage floor was the oil from tiny crankcase leaks. Now under the pickup and the Caddy ran a line of white ichor dripped from radiator grills covered with smashed bugs. Locust ichor smells acid and bitter and—another alien insectile component for which Sammy didn't know a word. There's a word for it in the locust drone.

Sammy intended to wipe the incrustation from the floor, but the smell and the heat and the bending over persuaded her to wait. It was easily twenty degrees hotter outside of the garage. The Worse was yet to come. In a few weeks the wheat would ripen, releasing massive amounts of water vapor, changing this corner of Kansas into a steam bath.

No breeze on the walk to the house except that created by Sammy's long strides. She liked the wind; it shook the tops of the wheat in great green waves. The susurrus of the wheat was like the crash of tide at Uncle John's, where she grew up.

Lou came in an hour later, so brown as to be a Mexican. A locust, disputing him for the door handle to his tractor, bit him. It was a small trapezoidal wound in the meaty section between thumb and forefinger.

Just before sunset a wind arose in the southwest. The polarized bay window in the sitting room began popping and ringing with locusts. Sammy and Lou went to watch the massacre.

The green flash of sunset came, turning the wheat fields into the sea. It made the polarized glass transparent. Sammy drew back, fearing the locusts would swim through. A trilobite darted from Lou's clothes as they fell in an empty heap on the sea-green shag rug. It swam through the window and into the sea.

Sam picked up the empty clothes and closed the curtains.

METAMORPHOSIS NO. 48

Publius Ovidus Naso was the first anti-establishment writer. (Look Ms. Moore I can still write a topic sentence!) He was born on March 20 in 43 B.C. in Sulmo (nowadays called Sulmona). He received a knightly education, with finishing school in Athens. He began his career as a bureaucrat but abandoned the public life for poetry. His patron was Marcos Valerius Messala; the establishment poets Virgil, Horace, and Propertius all belonged to Gaius Maecenas. His first poems were the *Amores*. In 1 B.C. he published his *Ars Amatoria* for which he was later exiled. The *Ars* was a treatise on seduction—a subversive book aimed against the official moralizing of the emperor Augustus. It has many mocking references to the *personal* symbols of Augustus' reign. He followed the *Ars Amatoria* with a tongue-in-cheek recantation *Remedia Amoris*.

The *Metamorphoses*, Ovid's only hexameter work, is a fifteen-book poem on the themes of transformation and love. It begins with the Creation and ends with the deification of Gaius Julius Caesar. It illustrates Ovid's rhetorical brilliance, his mythological learning, and his poetic imagination. Because of the *Metamorphoses*, Ovid was considered a great scholar in the Middle Ages, and his work is a gateway to Greek and Roman mythology today. On the eve of its publication and at the height of his career (A.D. 8), Ovid was summoned by Augustus.

Augustus banished Ovid to Tomis on the Black Sea. He was separated from wife and property. His crime was High Treason. He had written the *Ars Amatoria*.

Tomis had few Latin speakers. Ovid spent his life writing poems to the Emperor and successor Tiberius for a reprieve. Many have accused Ovid of knuckling under. This is not the case. In his *Tristia* he wrote a long poem declaring that the Emperor has no power over poetry. Poetry was the only cause he risked life for.

Although it was never home, Ovid became interested in Tomis. He wrote a local history and even composed poems in the local language, Getic. He died in 17 A.D.

The first book popularizing the flush toilet was *The Metamorphosis of Ajax* by Sir John Harrington, a godson of Queen Elizabeth I. "Ajax" was a pun on "a jakes," a latrine or privy, and Harrington's *Metamorphosis* described and promoted the water closet. According to Roger Kilroy (in *The Complete Loo*, London: Victor Grollanz, 1984, p. 15) Queen Elizabeth had a W.C. installed and a copy of Harrington's book chained to the wall nearby.

During Mass on a December Sunday, winter fell in Sulmona. It shattered when it fell. As people left their churches, they gathered up large slippery pieces of it from the pavement. Young boys ventured up trees and shimmied up drain pipes for particularly choice pieces. Some had, of course, fallen into fountains and drainage ditches and become embedded in ice. A few beggars and atheists had been killed by the falling winter, but no one mourned them.

The people carried the fragments of winter home. Some chopped the pieces up and fed them to their dogs. The beasts became heavier, hairier, and fiercer—the worgs of the Pleistocene, not seen here for many millennia. Others fed the winter to their cattle, which became wooly mammoths. Others still, driven by Pleistocene nostalgia, invited the winter into their beds. They became uncouth cavemen and awakened with spears and hunger. The Ice Age began in Sulmona and spiraled outward to embrace all of Europe.

METAMORPHOSIS NO. 49

My friends (who include a mock armadillo) say that I am a man of irregular (but charming) habits. It was on the evening of the eighteenth as I lit the four votive candles which light my garret (actually a two-bedroom apartment in Lubbock, Texas) when I am not in the mood for electrical lighting, that someone knocked at my door.

Four loud knocks separated by whole-note rests.

I shook out the match having lit only one candle and, annoyed, walked through the golden dimness to my door. Through the spy hole I saw Bob. Bob writes Westerns. Once the *Kirkus Reviews* called him "Zane Grey on mescaline." He is otherwise a professional Texan easily spotted in twilight because of his black Stetson.

I let him in. Made small talk. Seated him in the blue vinyl rocker. Offered him some spice tea. He accepted.

My spice tea consists of four cups oolong, one cup green gunpowder (which is a tea, not an explosive), one cup passion flower dried and chopped, and a tablespoon of cloves, allspice, cinnamon, nutmeg, and finely ground mandrake. One (heaping) teaspoon of the resulting mixture per cup and one for the pot and one for luck.

As the tea brewed I returned to my sitting room intent on dispelling darkness. Bob spoke from the shadowed rocker, "Yew still writin' them metamorphoses?"

"Yep."

"I got an idea for one. Wanta hear it?"

"Sure. Long as I don't have to pay you for it and don't have to use it."

I began lighting the second candle.

"Well as you know a lot of writers have written about characters gaining autonomy from text."

"Yeah." I went to the third candle.

"Well, suppose a character not only changes from one level

80

of reality to the other, but writes his author into the text—
trapping the tin-headed God, as it were?"

Out of the corner of my eye I saw Bob reaching for my pen.
I lit the entire book of matches and tossed it.

Bob went up like a firecracker, leaving a small pile of ash, my
typing still showing on some fragments.

METAMORPHOSIS NO. 50

Having come to see the universe as a chiaroscuro, where he
couldn't see the forms that cast the shadow or emanated the
light, Paul decided to exit the same. At a bad movie one can
always tramp down the carpeted aisles and demand a refund in
a loud voice. However, since Paul wasn't sure how to contact
the management or even in what coin the refund would come,
he chose an exit which might at least distract and amuse the
other bored patrons. Draw their attention away from the
flickering screen.

Paul locates the perfect exit. The highest floor of the Hyatt
Regency O'Hare Hotel. The interior is a vast well, an atrium
full of sound and plants. Demographics indicate the optimum
time for exit—five minutes before noon on Friday.

On Wednesday he rents a room conveniently nearby, carrying in his luggage two gallons of premium gasoline tightly
stoppered and a gallon of generic pink dishwashing soap. The
soap smells of roses.

He carefully makes happy conversation with his friends,
hoping to create a greater sense of impact.

On Friday morning after maid service he lays out a large tip,
the address of his Chicago flat, and a large yellow bucket.

He blends the gasoline and soap into a sticky pink gum. With
a painter's care he covers his face hands chest belly genitals
legs. The gum irritates his skin—he smiles. Under other con-

ditions he would have said it burnt him.

He pours the remaining gallon of goop over his head; it puddles onto the carpet. He runs snatching up the disposable lighter from his vanity with his left hand.

Through the carefully ajar door he runs to the balcony. As he leaps he lights the lighter, becoming a fireball.

One of the Forms casting shadow, the Management of the movie house, notices his departure. A great black tongue appears in midair, wraps Paul like a fly and removes the tasty morsel to the unseen mouth. No smoking in the theater. No one in the hotel has looked up.

Twenty-eight seconds later the lighter hits the tile below and is pocketed by a passing teenager.

METAMORPHOSIS NO. 51

Prohibition in the dusty streets of West Texas. The laws have come in and dried. Lemonade served at the yellow Amarillo Hotel. Coffee and tea at the AJ Ranch. Fellow can get mighty dry these days.

Carl spits his phlegm, red with the dust that comes off the canyon walls. Thought that cowboying would be an easy life. Shit. Spent three years pulling mesquite scrub from the ground before he could even touch a horse. Spend winter keeping the cattle in the canyon and summer keeping 'em out. Just as well, always twenty degrees hotter down there anyway; although, there is a creek.

Carl reaches for his canteen and remembers it's dry. Need to ride over to the windmill and fill her up. So damn dry the cattle piss goes straight into the ground, no puddle. Every step a little puff of dust.

Carl dismounts. Stretches his legs. Sure hope Chargo brings some tequila with him. Be nice to sit on the canyon rim at twilight with the cool wind with coffee cups full of the tequila from Chargo's folks.

Carl walks to the canyon rim. Watches the creek, northern fork of the Red River. So cool. So wet.

Carl leans over the rim and begins to fall softly, swiftly. His bones feel light and dry, his nerves stretch and seed. He twists into a new form to ease his fall. The wind shifts, blows him back. The tumbleweed rolls across the plains.

The tumbleweed rolls through the dusty streets for years. Prohibition is repealed but no one thought to pour whiskey on the tumbleweed.

In 1960 a chance encounter with a wino where the Amarillo Hotel used to stand.

Carl? He's a guide now at Palo Duro Canyon which was the AJ ranch. Some folks say he drinks a bit.

METAMORPHOSIS NO. 52

The shrill insect music ends, hanging like a twist of silver wire in the air. I shut off the recorder. The big black men return to their work, hot and sweaty and hard under the watchful eye of Madame Thia. They sing their hoodoo songs transplanted from the Gold Coast to Carib soil. I wonder if Madame Thia knows they sing necrophile songs focusing on her porcelain body.

Madame Thia will invite me to the Big House tonight for dinner. She believes that I'm here because I want her lithe body, not for my musicology. Tonight she will make love with me. I will perform excellently. The erotic stimulus is the air conditioning in her house (and nowhere else on the island).

After dinner, after small talk carefully avoiding mention of her husband away on business at his Yokohama shops, she disrobes. Her body, porcelain white, is not as perfect as weeks of recording on the island had caused me to imagine it. On either side of her torso, like auxiliary breasts, are three fibrous tumors, new handholds for unimagined sexual unions.

I take her violently on the satin sheet bed. My cock probing her grasping vulva. As we couple, the workers begin singing the song of spider necrophilia. As my partner's eyes facet and move I realize she is more intimately connected with her workers than I had thought. As we screw the six tumors lengthen into fine jointed black legs, her arms grow thin and dark.

Mating with the spider I prepare myself for the post-orgasmic prick of her fangs—the gentle loving consumption of my body.

METAMORPHOSIS NO. 53

Sheriff Bradley sez I got to make a statement concerning the fire and *why* it happened so here goes. It all started when I planted my beans y'all know those little redheaded sparrows just eat the hell out of unripened beans so I went to make me a scarecrow. Well I wanted something bright to sparkle and shine in the sun something for me to look at when I'm a-plowing the big field so I went to Arian Leher's house to fetch some of Mae's city clothes. Now yew all knew Mae some of ya more than others wildest one of Arian's daughters and all three pretty wild.

Well Mae fucked everybody in the county once and fucked some of 'em again in case they didn't know they was fucked the first time. And you know she finally took too many of them little yellow pills that city pharmaceutical salesman gave her cause yew was all at the funeral and yew all talked about it.

So I got a green skirt and brown top with sequins on it spelling M-A-E. I fixed it up nice and pretty putting the straw in all the right places. Sure liked looking at it on my way to the fields each morning always shining like she was happy with me.

Well one day I was walking back from some fence mending and a hot wind blew the smell of pussy to me. Now all you gents know there's nothing like pussy smell on God's green earth 'cept maybe that canned fish called salmon. He-he. So I looks around and the only woman is my scarecrow so I sez to it, "Well, Mae, I rekin you be wantin' some. It's been so long."

Well the scarecrow made a move to follow me all rustlin' like leaves in the fall. So we went into the house and made like man and wife. Towards midnight the scarecrow got up and slithered away. Well I wasn't surprised no bigger run-around than Mae Leher no sir.

Well no woman runs around on me so I went to my pickup and got my spare can of gasoline and headed after her. She was cutting across the wheat heading to that damned Tom Adam's. So I ran up behind her and doused her good and burned her proper which is how the fire got started.

METAMORPHOSIS NO. 54

The Eighteenth Century began, apparently, in the lush rolling years of the mid-1920s. It was finished in 1929 and shipped to Austin, Texas. I found it in 1985 for a dollar.

I was not the first person to have *The Eighteenth Century.* I guess the first person was an associate professor of English at the University of Pittsburgh named Joseph P. Blickensderfer who compiled the collection. I can only fault Mr. Blickensder-fer on the absence of one author, L. Sterne, my favorite eighteenth-century writer. He includes Daniel DeFoe, Jonathan Swift, Steele, Addison, John Gay, Pope, Boswell, Johnson, Thomas Gray, Oliver Goldsmith, and others. My favorite selection was from James Thompson's *The Castle of*

Indolence (1748). The first sentence of the seventy-fifth stanza is:

> Of limbs enormous, but withal unsound,
> Soft-swoln, and pale, here lay the Hydropsy:
> Unwieldy man! with belly monstrous round,
> For ever fed with watery supply;
> For still he drank, and yet he still was dry.

Meaty stuff there. *The Eighteenth Century* was purchased along with *The Short Fiction of Norman Mailer* and *The Blue Feather* by Zane Grey.

It has lived in Austin for fifty-six years, beginning as a textbook for the University of Texas. Its first owner was Raymond Slaughter who lived on Rio Grande and had somewhat flashy penmanship. For the summer course (in eighteenth-century literature) of 1931 it was sold to Ima Wilson who lived on Congress. Ima used the blanker pages for her notes from the class ("Heroic couplet—iambic pentameter—2 verses rhyming"). Ima has also carefully marked which selections to read ("A Modest Proposal") and which to omit (*Tale of a Tub*). Ima sold the book to George Moore who lived on campus (102 c L.C.D. ?) for the regular term. George didn't write in cursive. He abbreviated his name "Geo."

George hung on to his textbooks until the mid-1950s when he sold them to a used bookstore. The bookstore owner marked the endpapers (decorated with a map of eighteenth-century England) with "Antique $1.50." The book was purchased by an unknown person with a ballpoint pen.

Mr. Ballpoint Pen was primarily interested in William Collins and Thomas Gray (but skipped the former's *Persian Ecologues*).

Ballpoint boxed the book away with other cheaply bound twentieth-century editions, placed the box in his garage over his aging DeSoto, and died. The box was sold for 10¢ a book to a used bookstore on Research Boulevard (Highway 183).

Uncle Ovid's Exercise Book

I bought *The Eighteenth Century* for a dollar during the sale on anthologies. Anthologies are slow movers—I don't know why. I like anthologies.

The Eighteenth Century needed repair. Its book cover was coming loose. I tried soaking the cloth of the back spine with cynoacrylate ester (you know, the stuff for Krazy Gluing your head to the bottom of a steel girder). The old red cloth absorbed the glue and turned blackish red like clotted blood. But it didn't stick the book together.

Using packing tape, I bound the cover and spine internally and externally. The cover was cheap to begin with—its surviving fifty-six years is a miracle—but the paper is still good, although sepia-tinted.

When Ima Wilson owned *The Eighteenth Century* she was suffering from unrequited love for her professor. Ima sits in the front row writing notes with her No. 2 pencil. Ima frequently forgets her notebook and makes notes in the text—her interestingly mismatched eyes misted.

Ima sits and toys with her braids. Ima wears a severe blue dress that her mother made, but imagines herself wrapped in smoke-colored taffeta, a flapper gift-wrapped for her professor.

At night when it's cool and the breeze is off the Colorado River, Ima carefully copies the verse, "Ah me! Full sorely is my heart forlorn," onto a back flyleaf of *The Eighteenth Century*. The verse is from William Shenstone's "The Schoolmistress" (rhyme *ababbcbcc*).

Ima sells her book after completing her study. Ima leaves the Texas Hill Country and heads north to the Panhandle to teach my mother elementary school lessons and wait for the Dust Bowl and Steinbeck reality. Ima dries up in the Panhandle and blows away like a tumbleweed. Round and around and around.

Ima has lost *The Eighteenth Century*.

Ima Wilson, I love you.

METAMORPHOSIS NO. 55

Begin with view of New York City from the Hudson. Sunfall in chemically-enriched browns and reds. Orange light reflecting off the windows and anodized bars of the taller buildings. The fountain in front of the Metropolitan Museum reflecting blood. Neon lights flickering on both red and beetle-belly green.

A strange cloud, a column of smoke forms over mid-island. Drifting elongating gray and spectral. Slowly a forehead and eyes emerge, a wan New England face bringing to mind half-glimpsed fungi growing in Vermont woods during last summer's vacation.

Thin lips aristocratic nose. His eyes, yards and yards across, survey the city with blue hatred.

No one looks up as his shadow falls on the Chrysler Building on the Empire State on limousines departing Wall Street.

Rising city air passes through his neck and out through his lips in a sibilant hiss, words possibly hidden in the white noise. A single rooftop watcher in Greenwich Village recognizes the face. Quickly he rushes downstairs to his fifth-floor flat and checks the photo printed on the back of his copy of *The Mountains of Madness*. H. P. Lovecraft, New England fantasy writer. He tries to think of someone to call and his eyes light on the Polaroid.

He rushes back to the rooftop. Mr. Lovecraft's much more solid now although cadaverous and elongated as though seen through a fisheye lens. Its lips seem to move. It speaks.

". . . it is the Fate of mankind to be replaced by a hardy coleopterous species . . . ."

Suddenly thousands, millions of New Yorkers fall to the ground and begin to scuttle. Thin black legs sprout on each side, antennae growing from their heads. Carapaces form, as bright as IRT graffiti-covered cars.

Lovecraft vanishes. The Change has begun.

METAMORPHOSIS NO. 56

a polemic a prediction and a pineapple

How many times have you encountered this formula, "All women are one woman," either explicitly or implicitly, in a work of modernist or post-modernist fiction? Many male writers avoid dealing with women as persons by invoking the Great White Goddess. Mr. D. H. Lawrence is particularly guilty. Mystic gloss is stereotyping of the worst kind—not only does it depersonalize, but it enables the writer to claim understanding of the Eternal Feminine. Wheel those statues back to the basement, boys! It's time for the Archetypes Anonymous meeting.

Exactly seven years after you read this, a new type of street person will appear. They will dress as businessmen and women, but two features will set them apart. Their skin will be the red shiny metal of Classic Coke cans and their eyes will be solid black unblinking charcoal. They will answer no questions. They will stand on street corners, in theatre lobbies, and in queues for public transportation. Many questions will be asked about them: Where do they get their money? Where do they live? Where do they come from? Why are they here? Why are they silent? Police will watch them unendingly, waiting for them to transgress the law so they can be taken in for questioning. Police will be unnerved at the redfolk ability to slide out of their sight. The redfolk will be seen everywhere from DeKalb, Georgia to Ulan Bator, Mongolia. Much will be written about them, much more televised, and more still spoken in the quiet of night. Most people will come to regard the redfolk as angels. Crime, divorce, drug use will decline. Guilt and suicide will be at an all-time high. Five years after their arrival, the redfolk will congregate in front of the Chrysler Building in New York. They will gently eject the building's people. The Chrysler Building will rocket silently into the sky.

Twyla Tharp, choreographer and dancer, has come to Manhattan Beach, California for a vacation. Each morning between dawn and ten she dances along the beach. She dances the dances of *The Catherine Wheel.* Her rapid feet awaken an elemental. The sandy-eyed gnome utters an incantation. A greenish yellow smoke rises from the sand. It clings to Twyla. She pirouettes, the fog wraps around her like cotton candy. She's lost in the swirl. The next day a giant pineapple is found on the beach. Twenty-five feet tall, eleven feet wide. Foot-long vaginas are found among the textured surface. They open at night, emitting a golden light. The pineapple becomes a terpsichorean shrine. Thousands come nightly to dance. The elemental seeks another home.

METAMORPHOSIS NO. 57

Jerked by taboo and tea, Michael hides his face behind a white porcelain cup. It was Understood that one Did Not Speak of the Incident(s). And now the lady anthropologist friend of Jessica's had asked how he turned into a crane.

Michael is a *heyoka.* Michael is a contrary. Michael is a clown.

When Michael was fourteen he took a bag of tobacco and went to the rock ledges of the Dakota badlands on a dreamquest. On the second day he dreamed of lightning striking the mesa. Bad news for his family, he is chosen by the thunderbird. Much power mixed in with his destiny, the contraries move with strange angular momentum in-and-out of tribal orbits.

Jessica came to the Sioux lands looking for something exotic—a copper-skinned playboy. Many Sioux cowboys sleep with her but none go with her. The Spirit-within-Michael speaks and like a contrary like a clown Michael goes with her. Michael is a *heyoka.*

Now the lady anthropologist asks her question. Michael

does not know how to answer.

At a party where Jessica takes him the Spirit moves him. He changes into a great white crane and flies around the room. Some see a great white crane, others see a crazy Injun flapping his arms and levitating wildly.

This makes him no longer Jessica's playboy.

Jessica puts him in the third floor of a five-story walk-up near Columbus Circle. She pays the rent. Michael goes to Central Park and teaches ghost dancing and power dancing, and those who can see him learn.

Some see Spirit leaving him returning. Others see crazy Injun passed out too much firewater. This is the way of the white people's misunderstanding.

Before he answers the lady anthropologist's question he remembers the dreams that make him *heyoka* that make him clown that make him contrary. He remembers lightning striking again and again and filling him with great power.

And he becomes a lightning bolt. Snakes across the room and enters the womb of the lady anthropologist. He will engender a son to teach the white people new dances or blow away the dust of their cities.

Far above the world of men the thunderbird is pleased.

METAMORPHOSIS NO. 58

Maybe he should eat something. Blood sugar felt a little low but he wasn't hungry. Wasn't sleepy either. He thought of the Zen master who could eat when he was hungry and sleep when he was tired. It was a measure of enlightenment. He wasn't enlightened enough to know if he was tired. Mail won't be in for at least half an hour. If the guy's on time. If the relief girl— can't call her a woman, something about her attitude—is making the run, she'll be here in fifteen minutes. But she's so slow in sorting the mail. He'll go get a couple of carrots.

He'll try a writing exercise. He'll write, "After the initial shock, cellophane triggers off an immediate search for haircut or order to reduce the shampoo inherent in any uncertain situation. The mother is an unusual increase in our stegosaurus, coupled with a readiness to assume causal fauns where such connections may appear to be quite nonsensical. While the manticore can be extended to include such small details or such remote wiring that it leads to further confusion, it can equally well lead to fresh and creative pickles of conceptualizing reality.

"A cat who is confused is likely to jump to conclusions by holding onto the first apparently reliable belladonna of evidence that he detects through the fog of his stegosaurus. This, too, can be turned to positive advantage. The famous cellophane faun has developed it into a sophisticated therapeutic intervention called the Haircut Technique. He describes its manticore as follows:

> *One windy day . . . a shampoo came rushing round the corner of a pickle and bumped hard against me as I stood bracing myself against the wind. Before he could recover his wiring to speak to me, I glanced elaborately at my watch and courteously, as if he had inquired the mother of day, I stated, "It's exactly ten minutes of cat," though it was actually closer to 4:00 P.M., and walked on. About half a belladonna away, I turned and saw him looking at me, undoubtedly still puzzled and bewildered by my remark.*

Mail's in. He goes down. The postwoman says, "I've got a package for you, Mr. Bowen. I'm glad you came down." He says, "Thanks," bugged by the implication. He collects the white cardboard package along with a brown manila envelope and two newsprint flyers from the local supermarkets. He hurries up the stairs. He almost lost the flyers en route—it was a windy day. The brown envelope contained his story, "The Bradford Contract" and a typed rejection slip from Martin Z.

Odois of *Good Doctor* magazine. Martin said, "Dear D.B. Thanks for letting me see 'The Bradford Contract,' which I came across in the slush pile, where it had been lurking, away from human ken. It's got some funny stuff in it, but seems too surrealistic for *GD* to me. Yes, I know, . . . to walk a line between acceptable and unacceptable amounts of absurdism, and here you fall off . . . Good luck iwht (or "with" for you stuffy conservatives) it elsewhere, Best, Martin."

Saddened, but not crushed, he made a note to send "The Bradford Contract" to *In The Zone*. He is puzzled by the rejection. It had come on a carbon paper form. He had received the original and the pink copy.

He starts to return to his reading of *Meningitis* by Yuriy Tarnawsky. He remembers the package. He gets a knife from the kitchen. The package is from Carroll Wayne Watts Company. CWWC is a special place hovering in between the occult curios of Marlar and the industrial/military surplus of Jerry Co. The package contains an automated coin bank—a tiny black plastic coffin, when a coin is placed on the wreath a tiny glowing skeletal hand reaches from the coffin and snatches it away—a trio of refrigerator magnets, painted as rainbow trout, and Dr. M'abuse's See-All set. This last item was a small cardboard box (red and yellow with instructions printed black) holding a tiny vial, apparently full of quicksilver.

He knows Gisele, a stone fox of a programmer, gets home at 4:00. He'll use the stuff at 4:20. Currently it is ten minutes to two. He feeds his cat, does the dishes, and finally sits down to read. He has forgotten the five thousand perfect words he promised himself for today.

His answering machine beeps at 3:15. He'd dozed off. He'd been dreaming of fighting off a stegosaurus in a Max Ernst jungle. He listens to the message. His son is going to play baseball after school.

He starts coffee. He wants to be fully awake by 4:00. Maybe he can get some work done by then. No, he's still too muggy. He doubts if he knows five thousand words. The brew cycle is over. He picks up the glass carafe. He has forgotten to put coffee in the machine. He pours out the hot clear water and turns off the machine. He decides to shower and shampoo.

At 4:00 he leaves his apartment and walks to the Oxford Towers where Gisele lives. He arrives at 4:17. He buys a Coke from the vending machine near the laundry. At 4:23 he smashes the vial against the building. A patch of transparency spreads rapidly. Bricks, beams, carpet, clothing, all nonliving matter becomes as clear as glass. The apartment towers seem to have vanished, leaving ten floors of naked people floating in mid-air. Gisele lives on the third floor.

She'd known something like this would happen ever since she had met Bowen in the elevator. She is prepared. She touches the juju on her charm bracelet and is instantly changed into clear cellophane. She won't give the fat writer any cheap thrills. Unfortunately the window of her flat is open. Gisele is sucked out by the wind. She flies high into the air. She can see all of the city.

She becomes entangled with a kite line. Her juju is cut away while she attempts to free herself. She cannot change back without it. She cannot scream.

D. B. Bowen's son Mark helps the little kid get his kite down. He pulls the cellophane off the line. He wads it up and throws it in the closest garbage can. The kid thanks him. Mark goes over to the baseball diamond to wait for the guys.

METAMORPHOSIS NO. 59

We kept him with the rest of the Greeks because he spoke their language. We were never sure of his nationality or sympathy. He had no papers and claimed to have left memory behind on the island in his carpentry shop.

His eyes were Dorian green. His hair flaxen. He was a faun.

He spent most of his time on the exercise yard which overlooks the Aegean watching the crashing waves with sad green eyes. Because of his carpentry we called him Daedalus although officially he was No. 2091.

Unlike our other prisoners, he never gave us any trouble. Never complained. Never burnt himself on the electrified fence. Never wrestled with the guards.

Over the months he developed great carbuncles on his back and upper arms. His malady was an enigma. He began not wearing a shirt and sleeping on his stomach.

His last day he had spent hours tracing figures in the sand and finally lay upon the beach as though his cryptic labors had utterly exhausted him.

After several minutes of immobility I went to check him (and assure myself that no prisoner escaped through death when I was Officer of the Day).

When I was perhaps three meters away I heard a ripping sound. White wings pushed their way through his cheeks. Beaks began pecking their way through the carbuncles spattering his designs with blood. Of a sudden they were free. A flock of seagulls. Bloody, they circled the prison once to cleanse themselves and flew out of my sight.

My official report read: "Today Prisoner No. 2091 attempted escape and was shot. Remains buried. No other incidents."

METAMORPHOSIS NO. 60

At Circus, Circus any drunk with $1.25 can appear on a huge screen a la *Shape of Things to Come* (movie, not book). So they paid and flashed themselves in the wonderful setting. They gonna snap tongue at him, that may even have been accurate.

The Circus, Circus crowd of depressed wives and kids and Las Vegas winos smelled the blue wolverine poppers. Amyl nitrite and musk. Promise of penetrated rectums and vaginas gone gamy and brain cells exploding in interior nova before the big brainless night. They smell the poppers and they see the poppers in his hand on the big screen. And they mob the booth almost before he draws forth his pine cone-tipped wand and she drops her clothes.

One of the winos hands him a plastic ivy wreath and he gives the wino a popper. The wino breaks the popper, the crowd roars. The wino runs out on all fours to bay at the neon night.

The first fuzz arrives, tipped off by the strange sensitivity the fuzz always has for the gnosis. The Maenads fall on them ripping them to bloody blue fragments.

He steps out of the video booth and the picture fades. Somewhere drum music and pipe music and syrinx music boils in. Some of the men shed their grease-caked wino clothes and are handed wolfskins. If you pass Calpurnia on the sacred run lash her barrenness away.

His faun eyes scan the old men. One is missing. His procession dances into the street. Onlookers come in dribs and drabs and finally a great peopled tide from the Sands and the Stardust and Caesar's Palace. Entertainers hoot and bray at their disappearing audiences and blue-haired matrons converge upon them to tear the eyes from the blasphemers.

There's a little adobe mission not far from the Strip where Sam, the oldest wino, sleeps. One day in '55 he drove in from New York en route to a deal in L.A. to lose everything to sleep in the mission in the gutters in backyard trampolines anywhere.

Dionysius' procession pauses in front of the mission. The god enters, smiles in Sam's bleary eyes. Waves his hand and Sam's pants fall, exposing dark-haired goat's legs. Someone presses a wineskin in the satyr's wrinkled hands. Others lift him onto a donkey liberated from the Las Vegas zoo. Silenus.

The procession disappears into friezes and vases and plays and poems.

METAMORPHOSIS NO. 61

"The girl smiled faintly see, to get the isolate monkeys to . . . I didn't think that . . . ordinary social function but they . . . I admit I lied . . . monkey of either sex approaches and tickles you, but I didn't aggressiveness which the other dead; I just wanted you finally by introducing monkey children . . . the necrophilia waste a surprise, introduced by the Cellophane Faun . . . these needed the isolate adults so . . . have felt guilty about isolates socialized . . . It's interesting were willing to trust me . . . Stephen Jay Gould . . . the principle . . . leave the house alive. It was demonstrated scientifically."

The Doctor stopped. His seventh glass of retsina and his eighth attempt to justify the Gernsback-Campbell experiment to his patients. He felt his outlines blurring, slipping into the cigarette-smoke-blue medium of the room. The four patients became clearer as if precipitates although he was dissolving. A pressure on his chest his face burning his skull burning. The diagnosis was spontaneous vampirism. One of the patients, a mousey girl with a faint golden mustache, fishes a long thin alabaster tube from her purse. Thought they were illegal she must've been to the Market.

She aims at the Doctor, the other end surrounded by her thin lips.

She inhales. With a sucking sound the amorphous Doctor is drawn in like a djinn to its bottle.

The four women join hands around the table. In the center one of the Doctor's Rorschachs, an inky bat. The light falling on the ink shifts subtly as though the image now absorbed all light. A blue nimbus forms on its lacy edges. It pulls the matter of the room the women the table the five chairs the smoke the light all into itself.

In another timeplace, a gaslit New Orleans, a shadow of a bat appears on a gray wall near the French Quarter. A tear of blood falls from the shadow. When the blood strikes the filthy

pavement a seedy malicious dwarf appears.
The small figure, yellow with disease or opium addiction, with his foreign beard, approaches a passerby:
"Hey, mista, wanta buy a dream?"

METAMORPHOSIS NO. 62

We were in a school complex of some sort. I was giving weapons to the revolutionaries. The weapons were spaghetti squash. Certain spaghetti squash could be eaten—others were taboo. If you cooked them long enough they looked like Jack-in-the-Box Pizza Pockets. Then they served as an antidote.

I had this AKM with a banana clip and everything, but it didn't have the real *heft* of an AKM. It was hollow. I carried it around. It scared everybody. I was always throwing the secretary out so I could talk to the commandant. There were long planning sessions.

Rose would drive up in her green Chevy pickup with a load of new squash. And you would drive up and pick up the pizza pockets.

in the second version:
You had eaten a raw squash. You had changed into a sculpture made of large marshmallows. The marshmallows weren't stuck together too well. There were gaps between them. They were very hard like styrofoam. You could still talk and breathe. You were in great pain. I saved you by feeding you pizza pockets. If I hadn't found you—the marshmallows would've fallen apart. Our enemy was the famous Cellophane Faun.

METAMORPHOSIS NO. 63

I would like to be a six-armed Hindu god. A blue-skinned bejewelled Kong to climb to the top of the Penzoil Plaza in Houston with the glass and steel bending under my strong hands like a warm washcloth. And the blue skin metabolizing strange drugs and unknown hormones from actinic light and rich petrochemical air. Climb to the very top like Batman and Robin, pausing on the way to visit with rich Houston lawyers who will warn me of the fabled dangers which lie in ambush on the top of the skyscraper: of white bone nests of the dreaded Roc and of black mother Kali who dances around a blood-filled cauldron.

Climbing with two arms and two legs, using others to snatch treasures from within the building: a man subdued before knowing me; a dyed blonde from Hollywood, the perfect glowing literary symbol, sought once by Donald Barthleme climbing another glass mountain; and a corporate mummy, an elder wrapped in miles of magnetic tape full of figures on the corporate holdings and wisdom of the company, whose dead lips are consulted by younger executives in times of financial crisis. With these three treasures, which I call Mom's Apple Pie, Baseball, and Chevrolet, I can proudly climb to the top in front of God and everybody.

I wait for the planes to come and shoot me. Fall at 9.8 meters per second per second for the better part of four seconds with a resounding echoing fall.

And lie dead on the street, a hindrance to traffic, until my Resurrection.

METAMORPHOSIS NO. 64

"Really, Miss Thing, you should cram your slimy pets back into whatever hole they crawled out of."

Slam. And Miss Tish flounced down to street level no doubt thinking that she had waged a successful argument. Bianca couldn't do without her boa. The snake gliding (slithy, love, slithy) over her sequined dress was the perfect phallic counterpoint. Little Chuckles the constrictor had won her first at Dirty Sally's dragshow and really where did Miss Tish think the money comes from. (Of course I call it Chuckles. What do you want—Fang?) Besides there was a show tonight and she had better shave those chest hairs off.

Later, after make-up and moving all the furniture to the walls (a girl needs her space), she turned up the record (Linda Rondstadt—it takes real balls to do Linda Rondstadt) and lipsynced. Chuckles began his number (Of course it's a male snake! How can you tell? 'Cause I like it.), gliding just above the false breasts. Bianca smiling and grinding her hips as though the snake were caressing her erogenous core.

During the bit she felt another sinuous twining around her legs. Don't freak out girl, it's only Miss Eve's boa from one flight down come up for company. A brave peek and it was. Being hugged by both snakes was divine (I wonder if Miss Eve would send Satan to the show with me?). Swirl and enjoy.

The shadows in the room near the furniture seemed ropy. Wait girl, they're ropy, there're snakes everywhere—the couch the chairs that silly old dress model that Miss Tish bought. Boas, cobras, nameless black and coral and brown and green snakes. Bianca back-pedals and trips.

With a great crawling they swarmed her. On her lips, her eyes, her private parts—everywhere dry scaly undulation. It lasts forever.

It stops.

She opens her eyes. Except for Chuckles' spiral on the couch no snakes. On her chest is a stone, a fire opal! big as an egg! scaled like a snake, each scale fiery and opalescent. Bianca stands, clutching the stone, holding it to the light. She regains her composure, her regal bearing.

She places the smooth dry egg opal in her mouth. Something moves hatches slides down her throat—a tiny snake. The tiny snake will live inside her, wrapping around her heart, spiraling through her bowels. Growing larger and larger, taking nourishment from her body until only her skin remains. Then the snake will slough off her skin and seek out others of its kind.

METAMORPHOSIS NO. 65

The live iguana stands between the plastic Jesus and the magnetic Mary on the sun-split vinyl dashboard. On the passenger seat the sun-faded dusty Tarot cards lie. Behind the driver's seat is the skeleton all flesh baked away save for the still-living eyes. It longs for nightfall.

The rusty red Ford crippled by its last flat tire lies seven kilometers from Bardo, Arizona.

With the passing of a hawk's shadow the bright green Volkswagon tops the hill. It sweeps past the Ford, its movement caught in the iguana's eyes.

In the next few minutes it will have traveled halfway to Bardo and then half that distance and then half that half and yet again. Never quite reaching Bardo. When night comes the skeleton will come behind them with the rusty scythe stored in the Ford's trunk.

And the smell of plastic flowers will change to the scent of fresh blood.

METAMORPHOSIS NO. 66

Uncle Ovid's Exercise Book was initially written in Lubbock, Texas between September 1983 and April 1984. It is being revised in Austin (with substantial changes) at the suggestion of Curtis White. Today is April 15, 1986. I'll not change this section. Last night American planes bombed "strategic" targets in Libya. Today war appears inevitable.

I'm giving a public reading on the eighteenth. I started to call up Paperbacks Plus and ask if the reading had been cancelled. Then I realized that was absurd—war wouldn't interfere. The sunlight doesn't look any different today. The traffic still hisses by.

I've always believed that destruction is necessary for creation. Why have all my Shiva-ite truths left me today?

War may not be the result of last night's raid. War may be only the dream of madmen. But I fear a large metamorphosis is unfolding: flesh erupting red jelly, mosques returning to rubble, ambulances blossoming fire.

The One God will hear—I figure God's got to hear—prayers from both sides for victory. God Himself may pray for deafness.

For His sake I'll remain still today. Jean Genet died today.

METAMORPHOSIS NO. 67

I was packing books for the International Book Program to mail to the Department of English, Shao Yang Teachers College, Hunan Province, China, when a two inch by five inch piece of paper fell from a book to the floor. It was part of a jacket blurb, browned and broken, smelling of old book acid. Its message in black 8-point Helvetica read:

by hostile eyes? Or was it true as the neighbors were saying too sympathetically, that poor Louise's nerves were going to pieces, that she was beginning to confuse fact with fantasy? Then she learned about Miss Brandon's strange and frightening diary.

Immediately *Uncle Ovid's Exercise Book* began to change into Miss Brandon's diary. Such a metamorphosis is not unusual. Stories run together. Merge. Change like a cloud. Cancel themselves as they go along.

Dear Diary—
I don't know how long the mad parson will keep me in this potting shed. I promised him I wouldn't tell anyone that he had donned the costume of the Scarlet Ghost to scare people away and cover up his murder of the Amsterdam art-dealer Herr Jan Goochlekunst. I don't think I can stand any more tinned spaghetti on toast. I resolved today to wrap my diary in a plastic garment bag and bury it in one of the parson's geranium pots. The plant will soon need repotting and my successor—one of the Village ladies, no doubt—will know the horrible truth. If only the parson wouldn't leer at me so when he holds the hedge clippers.

METAMORPHOSIS NO. 68

An exposed layer of oil shale, brown with hematite, muddies the swamp water and sepia-tints the thick-rooted grass. The strata beneath the shale are nonporous and all run-off from the mountains gathers here in the swamp.

Monty Henson owns the swamp. Almost half a section, Monty sunk his last nickel into it. On a vacation at a nearby resort Monty hiked over the mountains and saw the rainbow film on the puddles. Monty saw dollar signs in the film. He spent the remainder of his vacation in a dance of red tape to acquire the land.

The next summer he paid enormous fees eight times for geologists of varying stripes to tell him that shale oil is inaccessible. He lives in a rundown self-built cabin. His carpentry's good enough to bring in some scratch during the summer.

The varying geological tests left behind a large collection of fossils. Bits of club moss and fern wisps of permineralized pre-palms. Monty embedded them in the plaster of his sitting room: a silent stone garden. He is happiest in the bathtub—a solar water heater being his last big buy before bankruptcy—floating in hot oily swamp water, watching the stone souvenirs of the valley's rolling past.

In the winter he discovers his carpentry proved insufficiently insulated. The plaster-encased sitting room holds warmth and he remains most of the winter in the tub, like Marat.

The oily swamp water galls his skin. Vast scaly irruptions along his back. Pus and blood stain his clothes. He visits the healing woman of the valley, Fedalina.

The wrinkled *bruja* suggests—at least through his high school Spanish—to go to an entirely vegetable diet.

So like many other valley inhabitants he discovers the fat-building virtue of pinto beans. By late winter his back smells of rotting flesh and he begins to avoid the other valley inhabitants.

In the spring a tourist from the resort spots a brontosaurus on the Henson place.

The sheriff finally comes to investigate. No brontosaurus no Henson. Only the sitting room overgrown with the club mosses and palms of another era.

METAMORPHOSIS NO. 69

His parents told him that the scar on his right side was the reminder of corrective surgery on his liver. Rudy knew the truth. He was born with a Siamese twin. The surgery to separate them had only been partially successful. The other half had died.

During puberty he began to see his twin. At first he could only see him out of the corner of his eye. Even after months of practice he couldn't stare directly at his twin. The other would fade out avoiding his gaze leaving only a pain behind his eyes. He called the twin Hassan.

Hassan was always silent. He was built upon more beautiful lines. Dark eyes, cream skin, androgynous face, full cruel lips. Other people seemed aware of Hassan; they would step around him and often ask Rudy, wasn't someone else just here?

When he was fifteen, he began to talk to Hassan with his mind. He discovered that he shared tactile sensations with Hassan. He could walk up to a cute girl and enjoy copping a feel vicariously through Hassan. Caressing breasts, kissing thighs. The girls would giggle and blush, only subliminally aware of Hassan's presence.

One day at the video arcade, Rudy playing at Eliminator, a guy in tight jeans and leather jacket bent over the pinball machine on Rudy's right. Hassan stretched the invisible flesh link so he could fondle the guy's crotch.

Rudy was disgusted. He/they weren't queer. God how sick. Rudy turned to leave. Hassan grabbed a knife from the pinball stud. Hassan brought it down on the link, sawing through with three quick motions.

Rudy died. Hassan lives on in lovers' dreams and the blue movie circuit.

METAMORPHOSIS NO. 70

One of the oldest and best cons—as any Gnostic worth his heretical texts knows—laid on homo saps is the Babel con. "Separating the sons of Adam lest they build towers to heaven." (Modern architects beware!) It was laid on mankind by an old seedy con artist called Demiurge between the muddy waters of the Tigris and the Euphrates. Occasionally some bright boy will attempt to bridge the word lines. That's where I come in. I carry a badge. Dum de dum dum. I am an Angel hustling for Demiurge. Not a pretty job. Not even a safe one. Once I was imprisoned in a mirror by this hep cat named Solomon the Wise. I was just trying to pick up some ice to impress the local girls in an earlier time period (and there were giants in the Earth in those Days). And *pop!* there I was in the mirror. Anyway the bright boy I was after was a German bishop who shoulda known better I say—named Johan Martin Schleyer. In 1880 he develops an international language called Volapuk. It was pretty heavy with Anglic roots, simple and regular grammar and not nicely ambiguous like English or German.

The Chief calls me up, briefs me, assigns me. Other Angels will discredit it as "too Germanic" in the early 1890s relegating it to the domain of well-intentioned crackpots. My job—assassinate and replace Schleyer.

Outside the bishopric I weave a body out of light. I form myself into Jack Webb down to the 714 badge number. Angel's inside jokes usually refer to future events, impresses the marks decades later. The events are not really "future" at all—just depends on how you look at the Minkowski plane but that's a trade secret you know.

So I tug the bell pull. Bishop's valet answers. I tell him I'm from the *New York Sun* and want to do a story on Volapuk and would he get the Bishop?

I'm shown into a tacky German attempt to imitate a tacky

Victorian drawing room. I compose myself, consulting my notes in an internal mirror.

The Bishop comes in, extending both hands in greeting. I rise grab both hands focus on my reflection in his eyes feel the crack of soul-transfer at the base of my neck. Surely you've seen the Hanged Man Tarot trump? And I stand in a dark cassock looking at a terrified Jack Webb.

Jack Webb, formerly the Bishop, throws himself on me. I scream for Franz, my valet. Franz bursts in and fires. Jack falls to the parquet floor.

OK that's the story—now will you please break this gem and release me?

METAMORPHOSIS NO. 71

Now EtherHead was given a prettier and more acceptable name but I won't give it to you cause he has a sister who's an up-and-coming jazz harpist. EtherHead was a huffer, the bottom of the drug culture. Huffers are lower than goofball artists or Valium purse snatchers. They'll do anything to get off. Usually they hitch onto a no-pay lousy-hours job for easy access. Working late shift at a plastics factory or a refinery. Sniffing all kinda polymers when the foreman ain't watchin.

EtherHead was the night janitor at Arkham Charity Hospital. In one of the rooms he swept was a brown glass bottle labeled Ether and Alcohol. Now a little ether goes a long way. Ether-Head would dampen a cotton swab, wrap it in wax paper and stick it in his lunch box. He musta found or stole the lunch box—rusty model with Star Wars characters on it. I wouldn't trust EtherHead around my kids.

After work which meant 4 ayem EtherHead would sidle outta the Hospital and head up the hill to the cemetery. Dead folks hardly ever disapprove of the morality of the living and if they do they're tol'able quiet about it.

On his last day there was frost on the ground so he took a hospital towel along. He spread it out real nice over a tombstone in the Armitage family plot and sat. He unwrapped his treasure, stuck it in his right hand to warm it. Then he brought his hand up to his nose and huffed and held that breath. And again. And again.

Now ether takes your body away and has it send messages home by long distance. The messages will eventually crawl up to the brain but by that time they're not news.

So we was able to walk right up to him. By the time the message "Ghouls" reached his brain, we were already at work.

To transform a man to a ghoul is simple. We needed Ether-Head to suck the embalming fluid out of the corpses—most of us can't stand it.

METAMORPHOSIS NO. 72

He found himself after an indefinite interval of time on the Deluge Express traveling first class from Minraud to Carcosa. The porter stamped his ticket of a resilient silvery-iridescent metal with an octagonal punch. He rode in a Pullman Palace car—after an hour the white sand outside got tiresome.

He made his way toward the front of the train to the ice viewing car. Here the railroad maintained a car refrigerated at minus one degrees Celsius. It was filled with ice sculptures of fantastic animals. For those jaded passengers particularly tired of the desert, one of the cars had a cosy corner of Victorian delight with ice blocks tinted various pastels, and blowtorches were provided.

His favorite study was a great dragon carved of blue ice. It would measure three meters if laid straight; however, it curled into the sinuous "8" of infinity—its many-toothed jaws almost closing on its diamond tail. Far more care had been lavished on its creation than on its fellows—a unicorn, a peryton, and a hedge-hound. Each scale, no bigger than a quarter, was perfectly shaped. The talons, ranging from two centimeters to twenty, curved viciously away from the paws. The lidded eyes had tiny lashes, each of a single prismatic ice crystal.

He watched the dragon for many hours. His limbs grew white with cold. He ran his hand along the creature's icy spine. Startled, the dragon bit his hand, munching three fingers.

By the time he arrived in Carcosa he had quite forgotten the incident.

METAMORPHOSIS NO. 73

Lewis and Clark said, "The Great American Desert is uninhabitable." Well I'm not inhabiting it, I'm floating above it. Or rather the steel chair I'm sitting in is floating. It maintains a stationary position with regard to the desk and to the earth, which is eleven meters below. The chair and the desk are in the same relationship to one another as if I were sitting in my office. It is my desk. I do not remember how I came to be floating here. It's spring. It's the Texas panhandle—near Bushland I would guess. Whatever grace supports the desk and the chair doesn't extend to me. I throw copper paper clips onto the three-awn, sideoats grama, switchgrass and wild rye. I feel bad about littering the sideoats grama—it's our State Grass.

I can move off the chair and dangle or I can stand on the desk. Too high to jump. They must be missing me at my office. Who will feed my cat?

At the furthest righthand corner of my vision I can see a strip of highway. Cars come by every few minutes. I've tried shouting and waving but they don't respond.

It's morning. The desk, chair, and I cast the shadow normally expected. I can detect no wires or supports.

In my righthand top drawer are four #10 envelopes, three #11 envelopes, two IRCs, a stapler, a company phone book for 3M, a copy of *Afoot in a Field of Men* by Pat Ellis Taylor, and the *IEEE Bulletin*. The lower, larger drawer contains thirty files pertaining to my 3M work and one file containing thirty-seven pages of my epic poem *Mickey Mouse Eats Minestrone* in which Annette Funicello is revealed as the White Goddess. The central drawer contains forty-one paper clips, a nonfunctional calculator, three pens, two pencils, a seashell, and three-quarters of a roll of peppermint Lifesavers. There's a calendar/blotter on the desktop, a white telephone whose connections trail off into space, and a picture of my 1962 Mercedes Benz 220SE with personalized plates: Pel Terry.

I finish my inventory. The desk, chair and I begin to move. Very slowly. We move in the direction the chair faces. The breeze is nice. I'm floating over white-faced Angus cattle. Mainly cows and yearlings. The cows don't seem impressed by my transit.

There's a man standing in the field. He's wearing overalls and a gimme cap. He sights my desk in a very elaborate antique brass sextant. I yell at him and he waves with his left hand—never taking the sextant away from his eye.

I pass over a ranch house. No one's outside. Here come more cows. There's a man in this field. He's dressed as a British undertaker. He's holding out a plumb line. He watches the line's shadow very intently. He ignores my cries. As the desk passes over him, he drops the plumb line.

The desk begins moving much faster now. I suddenly can't move. I can see my right hand on the desk. My flesh is becoming granular. The grains are shifting. It's a light pleasant feeling. The desk has become granular. The grains are mixing.

My vision broadens, flattens. My eye grains spill through the mass of crystals. The crystals whiten. Color vanishes as grains become smaller.

The mass achieves order as a cube. Negentropy. The cube is

one-and-a-half meters on a side—flying smoothly despite the laws of aerodynamics.

The cube speeds toward a gigantic Delft coffee cup sitting on a gigantic Delft saucer. The saucer sits on the smoking remains of a smashed city. Icube plunge into the coffee.

METAMORPHOSIS NO. 74

Watching the pumps at Thirty-fourth and Queen gives a guy a lot of time to think. Out the glass—across the pumps—and the street—the AT&T building which had a running pattern of yellow, red and roan bricks. Because of the pattern and the convection waves rising off the brick, the building seemed to breathe slowly quietly regularly. Kelley liked to think it was breathing.

And why not? It sure had everything else an organism needed (Kelley prided himself on being a public TV naturalist). Food—brought in crumpled brown sacks by the employees. Water—from the big white pipes on the west side of the building. And with all those wires, even eyes and ears. Kelley kept his vitalist theories to himself 'cause the guys would think he'd been too near the fumes.

In high spring, during a lull, he got Crazy Eddie to watch the pumps and slipped across the street for a pint of chocolate milk. On his way to the store he gingerly patted the AT&T building.

It was breathing. Slowly. Regularly.

Kelley didn't get his milk. He went back to the station kinda quiet. He didn't notice the stain on his hand until quitting time when he washed up. One of the roan bricks had left a powdery mark across his palm. The Lava soap didn't touch it.

That night he tried all his household reagents—vinegar, rubbing alcohol, Lysol, mouthwash. He managed to inflame both arms up to the elbow, but the stain persisted. He stared at

111

his palm through the movie, the news, the Carson show with vague thoughts of cancer and leprosy. The late movie was *The Blob*. That cinched it.

Next morning he called in sick. He looked through the yellow pages for dermatologists and got one who could see him that day. The doctor's office was in the labyrinthine section of downtown guarded by one-way streets and confusing parking signs. Kelley had to park at a pay lot six blocks away.

On the nervous walk to the doctor's office his hand began itching like mad. Passing the gray brick face of the IBM building he paused to rub his hand. The roan stain rubbed off on the corner of the IBM. Kelley cleaned his hand, returned to his car, went home.

A few weeks later Kelley passes a new building downtown—a roan and gray brick affair next to the IBM. Kelley overhears a remark from a passerby:

"Strange how they just sprout up, isn't it?"

METAMORPHOSIS NO. 75

It was the day after the welfare checks and most of the Project was awakening to the challenge of their hangovers. On the plaza between the four buildings, by the waterless fountain, one ancient figure could be seen. Granpa McRansom, one of the many old people wandering in memories of their own choosing. McRansom's memory—at least for today—was the losing of his virginity.

He couldn't remember the girl's name or the date, but he remembered the occasion. It was the landing of men on the moon—long ago, in the last century, when he was nineteen and could get a hardon.

McRansom wore green government-issue overalls and sweater—the only distinguishing attire being a motorcycle helmet which had decorated the walls of his tiny flat for years. Had anyone been awake enough to watch him, they might have supposed it afforded some protection from the October frost.

The old man gathered scraps of paper, plastic, twigs, and twine in a small pile by the fountain. When the pile was six or seven inches deep he labouriously bent and mounded it about his legs. He fished a precious match from his breast pocket—striking it against the concrete.

He lit the debris pile and held his arms stiffly at attention. For some minutes nothing. Then the pile caught. Flames hissed around his legs. Flames shot out of his feet, lifting him a few inches from the pile.

For a heartbeat he hung there, and then he rose swiftly. In two minutes he was gone from sight.

METAMORPHOSIS NO. 76

It was there at No. 25 rue d. Dragon—which is a small prognosticator's shop between a repairer of reputations and a shop which sold relics of the future—that I was employed as a woodcutter and shopsweep. I would chop the wood, feed the stove (actually overfeed the stove, for the old Romany *chai* who kept me had thin skin and chilled easily), sweep the shop and make tea for those waiting their turn at my master's cartomancy.

On that morning I rose two hours before dawn, ate a simple breakfast of bread and cheese, and made my way to the fortuneteller's. Letting myself into the small back courtyard through a hidden panel in the fence, I grabbed my axe and went to the woodpile. The logs were frosted. I removed the top layer, which would burn unevenly because of the moisture. I uncovered a little old man sleeping in the wood. His clothing and complexion so nearly matched the wood that at first I took him for a pile of logs. I discovered my error when I bent to grab a log for the chopping stump and grabbed instead his leathery chin. I shook the old fellow roughly, bringing him around.

"See here, old man, it's time for you to leave. I've work to do."

"My son, I want only to sleep."

"Find a poorhouse or a mission then."

"No, no, this is my place."

"It's the gypsy's woodpile, stinking reprobate."

"It does nicely as a bed. You must thank your employer."

"Look here, old man—I'm a woodcutter and I'm going to start chopping wood and when I come to you I'll chop you into fourteen-inch lengths and feed you to the gypsy's stove."

"It matters not to me as long as I can sleep 'til then."

I went about my chopping—striking each log with great vigor and violence—hoping to scare the old man away. As I uncovered his chest and legs I moved more slowly than is my wont—seeking to give him time to consider my intent of slicing him (much as a child will, in giving an ultimatum to another child, when counting to the deadline, begin to insert fractions into the cardinal queue).

Finally the old man was completely uncovered, though still sleeping soundly. I lifted his body—surprisingly light as though he were made of wood—onto the chopping block. I raised my axe with the intent of bringing it down an inch or so from his head—scaring the reprobate to death, and then flinging him over the fence into the tiny shit-covered alley. A few beads of sweat—I told you I'd been giving great displays of vigor—rolled stinging into my eyes and clouded my vision. I brought the axe down on the crown of his skull, cleaving it open with a great bloody crack. Brain and blood splattered my wood. Something twitched inside the man's head and then sprang out increasing its size manyfold in the process.

A gray-eyed woman in blood-soaked and brain-spattered antique military costume regarded me with unearthly contempt. The old man rose from the chopping block. He closed the bone-lined vulva in his head and wiped the blood from his hands on his trousers. Arm-in-arm, the old man and the military woman left through the secret panel of my master's back fence.

Because of all this excitement, I was late in fixing my master's fire and was soundly beaten, as well you might imagine.

METAMORPHOSIS NO. 77

And it came to pass that the Magician was commissioned to place a curse on Rex Hatfield, an incompetent asshole. The Magician called upon Bitom, spirit of fire of the Enochian tablets. As smoke leaves fire let Rex Hatfield leave Ohio DataCorp.

And thus it came to pass that (choose your own ending):
1. Mr. H resigned because he felt "burnt-out."
2. Mr. H's house burned to the ground. Mr. H was within.
3. Mr. H's superior Mr. Z, a man of fiery temperament, dismissed him in a fit of rage.
4. Mr. H succumbed to lung cancer from the cigarettes he smoked.
5. Mr. H became obsessed with the inner fire and journeyed to India to study Agni Yoga.
6. Mr. H was seduced by a salamander at a local bar. When the salamander reached climax her body temperature increased to 1000 degrees Celsius. Only Mr. H's teeth remained.
7. Mr. H was challenged to a pepper eating contest by his Cajun brother-in-law, consumed twenty-three jalapenos, and expired.
8. Mr. H had the misfortune to stand between two mirrored glass Corbu towers on summer solstice and was vaporized.

9. Mr. H's wife Irene locked him in the sauna before departing to the Bahamas with her lover Raoul, and he melted.
10. Mr. H, saddened by his losses on the stock exchange, climbed the unused incinerator smokestack at Ohio Data-Corp and leapt to his death.
11. Mr. H was demoted to company cook and decided that he couldn't stand the heat and left the kitchen.

The ways of Bitom are mysterious.

METAMORPHOSIS NO. 78

(IN HOMAGE TO JEAN FERRY)

In the summer of '83 I was overtaken by fatigue. Tiredness exhaustion futility boredom. Born from the heat and the lack of literary sales and the gradual melting together of heretofore discrete elements in the alembic of my life. In my fatigue I had fallen into the custom of allowing my discarded manuscripts to pile up—telling myself the following lies:

A. I am a great *bricoleur* and will use the discarded manuscripts (and the junk mail which also infested the pile) in numerous cut-ups and collages which will astound the literary world.
B. I will contribute my papers to a public library and effect a great tax savings.
C. I will purchase one of those ingenious devices which turns waste paper into firegrate-size logs and give these to friends with fireplaces with the coming of winter (as a corollary to this lie I told myself I would develop friends with fireplaces by wintertime).

The yellow texts (I write my first drafts on legal pads) formed a multi-strata mini-mountain behind my desk. The pressure and weight of the sediments began the lithic and metamorphic processes that sediments are heir to.

Upon entering my writing room on the morning of August 1, I spied a little yellow man. At first I thought he was an Oriental because of his complexion, but closer examination revealed his skin color to be that of pale urine and I knew he was born of the pile of manuscripts. His eyes, like great black pearls, consisted of the ink from my ballpoints, flairs, computer printer. He had taken great care in his genesis—so much so that not a single loose manuscript was left and the room was its most pristine since I'd moved in.

The little man said nothing but looked at me quite knowingly. And why not? Every word I'd written in months had become his flesh. Attempting to overcome my fatigue I summoned three plans:

A. I would bundle him in a garbage bag (my wife and I certainly couldn't afford another mouth to feed) and deposit him in the tan Dempsey Dumpster in the alley.

B. I'd give him a quill (or perhaps a brush; he still seemed Oriental and I'm fond of Japanese calligraphy) and let him write himself to death. After all, he could only have as many words as I had put into him.

C. I would take art classes at Texas Tech and learn the craft of molding papier-mâché. I'll mould him into a more agreeable form—say a large dog or perhaps a family of cats—and give these pets to friends who wished animal companionship or perhaps to a public home for animal waifs.

But alas! so great was my fatigue I did none of these. Each day he watches me with horrible knowing eyes. I do not love him like a son, but fear and loathe him like a curate to whom I've made a terrible confession.

My wife is much luckier than I because she cannot see him and can enter the writing room without fear.

METAMORPHOSIS NO. 79

The dying centaur tries to con me into making a charm from its blood. My great-aunt on my mother's side got taken in by that. I just smile as the centaur wheezes out blood and bits of lungs. The lungs are pretty scrambled, the 30-.06 entered just left of the breastbone. They're yellow too. Must've been a cigarette smoker—looked pretty funny in a Seven-Eleven if you ask me. I wouldn't let one in my store. Takes all types. Three more gasps and its over. Jake grabs the hindlegs and I get the forelegs and we drag the body through the scrub oak back to the pickup. The critter weighs 800 pounds easy. Hope the winch'll hold. 800 pounds at 50 cents a pound divided by 2 comes to 200 dollars, less 35 for the license and maybe 10 or 20 for the gas and the ammo—ain't bad for a morning's work.

Jake points out that Japanese and Frenchmen think centaur meat is a delicacy. Damn near turns my stomach at a time like this when you can smell the blood. Try haulin' this mother to Japan, I say. We both laugh. We lay the body down for a breather. At least you can see the truck from here. White Chevy Custom Ten. Don't know what's custom about it. Jake hands me some Wintergreen Skoal. I take a pinch. Never cared much for wintergreen. Reminds me of that pink medicine you take for the runs.

Kind of timidly I ask Jake if he wants the head. He smiles and says no you take it. I think it'll look good over the mantle. Mildred's liable to squawk though: Well let her, she don't know how dangerous shooting these critters is. A lot of 'em have blow guns with poisoned thorns and got treaties on the side with satyrs. Of course, I checked with the local N.R.A. office. There's not *supposed* to be any satyrs in Balcones Woods. Once you hear the pipes you're a goner.

I saw one of them back in the V.A. hospital. One of the ones who's heard the pipes. He'd just wander around wide-eyed and sometimes he'd walk into a wall. Might as well have scrambled eggs for brains.

Jake shrugs and I shrug and we start dragging the body again. It's getting a lot of leaves and thistles in its hair but the taxidermist will be able to fix that. I'd better get the people at the dog food place to drain the blood from the head when they cut it off. Glad I bagged—at least I think it was my shell and not Jake's—a male. The game warden's got your ass if you get a mare. I'm beginning to think this sucker weighs 900 pounds. My calves hurt and there's a pain on my left side just below my heart. I had to be the one—Jake couldn't hit the broad side of a barn.

We clear the scrub. Easier going in the tall grass. Jake's got a little blood on him. We stop and clean it off with a hanky and then he throws the hanky away. The blood's poisonous if mixed with sweat or saliva unless you can take some mandrake. I've got some atropine drops in my first aid kit, but like a jackass I left the kit on the dining room table. I'll ask the people at Alpo's for a couple of drops just in case. You can get real drunk on atropine and beer. I forgot the damn beer too.

Jake asks me if they pay in cash or check. I've never traded with these folks but the plant near Plainview pays in cash. The grass's still wet with dew and the carcass just slides along now. It's warmed up a bit since we shot the thing. We got a couple of big black flies trailing us zzzzz zzzzzzzzzzzzzzzzzz (smack)— Jesus Christ how can he slap a fly right onto his shirt like that. I'm gonna lose my cookies between the blood and the fly guts and this goddam wintergreen snuff. He don't even wipe it off. What a pig.

Finally at the truck. Jake starts up the engine and the little compressor on the back gets to whining. I fix the hook right where the left foreleg joins the body. I sure hate to tear up the beautiful appaloosa coat, but Mildred don't want it and Jake's old lady don't even know he's off hunting. Jake starts up the winch. And he jumps up in the back and grabs the shoulders and I push on the butt which is really disgusting 'cause it emptied itself when we shot the mother. Most of the shit's been wiped on the grass. Damn I'll be glad when I can have a shower. I push and Jake pulls and the compressor sounds like it's going to blow something and my heart sounds like its going to blow and the zzzzzzzflieszzzzzzzzzarezzzbackzzzzzinzzzzzazzzzzsextetzzzzz and finally it's in the pickup.

Pickup's a lot lower on its shocks. Maybe it weighs 1000 pounds.

Jake shuts off the compressor. I walk away from the zzzzz and pant like hell. I promise myself *this* year I'm going to start that aerobic program that Mildred's been touting. Spit out the snuff.

Jake walks up. He's got a thermos from the cab. He offers me a cup of coffee and I wash my mouth out. It scalds but it's clean. I spit the coffee out and pour myself a cup for drinking.

Jake gets him one too. It's gonna be a hot one. We shrug. We both want to get the body to Alpo's before it starts to smell. We walk to the cab. I'll drive. I turn on the air conditioning and roll up the windows. Jake unfolds the map. He'll navigate.

I have to take the dirt road pretty slow since the shocks are so weighed down. Even so we scrape bottom two or three times even before we hit the stream ford. If I gotta pay for a new oil pan it'll eat into my profits pretty deep. Damn Jake wouldn't offer to pay half either. He hasn't shelled out a nickel for gas. I think when it's time to fill up the truck I'll just pull into a gas station and say it's your turn old buddy with no preamble. He'll probably pay then.

We splash through the ford. I can see speckled trout in the stream. I came down here last year to fish and didn't see a damn one. It's about a mile to the highway. Jake's been real quiet.

I look over. He's as white as a sheet and his forehead's terrible swollen. Oh Jesus he's got a little blood in him. Probably through that damned snuff. He looks like he's about to puke. I stop the pickup. I get out and walk around to his side. I open the door and sure enough he pukes all over my shoes.

Come on bud. I help him to the creek and wash him off and

fix him a cold compress. I set him down in the shade of a cedar tree. I tell him to rest. I'll get him a couple of aspirin and drive down to the warden's cabin for some mandrake extract. He just nods.

As I walk back to the pickup I hear his clothes rip. I wheel around. His swollen forehead sprouts a horn.

I fire up the goddamned pickup fast as I can. I tell the game warden about Jake. He gives me the Balance of Nature speech. Alpo's ain't open yet but the Seven-Eleven is. I'm going to drink eight or nine beers and then call Mildred.

METAMORPHOSIS NO. 80

The Pyramid Builder

CHAPTER I

In this chapter John Rothe is revealed to be all things to all men. To Charlotte Ubu, leading Denver feminist, he is a genial uncle. To the Chamber of Commerce, he is Denver's leading banker. To the Diocese, he is financial and spiritual pillar. He is even a patron of the arts. At the end of the chapter he receives a call from his lawyer Yage Thomas. The gig is up.

CHAPTER II

In this chapter young John Rothe is born in the silk stocking row of Carson City. His family's money protects John from the harsh realities of the Depression. In 1938 he receives a camera and a wirerecorder. With these he is able to supplement his income through blackmail. After the first blackmailing scheme, his uncle Abramelin Rothe denies his nephew access to his (Abramelin's) gardens. John will wonder how the old man knew for the rest of his (John's) life. As an amateur reporter for the *Carson City Tattler,* John learns the importance of publicity. Throughout his life there will be many, many photos. He stares hard at the camera, willing himself to be remembered. See? Here he is now.

CHAPTER III

In this chapter John meets Father Sustare. John's folks are glad John is so interested in the Church. Father Sustare introduces John to sodomy. John graduates from high school. Rumors begin about John's "religious life."

CHAPTER IV

Yage Thomas, a third-year engineering student at the University of Cairo, is initiated into the mysteries of the dark side of the Tree of Life. In the Anti-World he gains a glimpse of John Rothe and the fate lines glimmering around him.

CHAPTER V

Don Trampier, young homosexual millionaire from Boulder, Colorado, arrives in Cairo to make *Passion Among the Pharaohs.* He gathers *gali-gali* men, snake charmers, and plump belly dancers for "color." Anti-American sentiment sweeps Cairo with the arrival of Rommel's army. Yage Thomas enables Don to narrowly escape, but all the film equipment is lost. In an obscure ritual in Malta, Yage and Don place a curse on Don's wealthy grandmother. They return to the States—Don to Boulder, Yage to Yale Law School.

CHAPTER VI

John becomes a male nurse. During the day he works at Our Lady of Sorrows Charity Hospital in Boulder—at night he's a private nurse to Mary Trampier. Don arrives from Egypt.

CHAPTER VII

John becomes a procurer of underaged boys for Don. There are larger and larger parties. There is a raid. John posts a twenty-five dollar bond and leaves for Denver. Don leaves for Europe on V-E Day. Yage begins his practice in Boulder.

CHAPTER VIII

Mary Trampier dies, leaving all her wealth to Don in a "spendthrift" trust. He'll be able to live opulently, but never get his hands on the capital. Yage Thomas lends John enough money to begin an X-ray lab. On August 6, 1945, Father John Sustare is consecrated Bishop of Denver.

CHAPTER IX

Two years pass. The world recovers from war. The Marshall Plan. John's clinic flourishes. John buys a restaurant and the Starlight Motel. An incredibly emaciated Don Trampier turns up at Denver General Hospital. By means of the folding green passport, John spirits him away to the Starlight.

CHAPTER X

John assumes control of Don's life as "business manager." The drinking is curtailed. The parties begin anew. John buys Don's trust for Don's "own good." Sister Mary St. John becomes Bishop Sustare's private secretary. Don's physical and mental health return.

CHAPTER XI

John begins dipping into the trust with the aid of Yage Thomas. Money is stored by Bishop Sustare in tax-free Church funds. John and Yage become fiduciaries for the Bishop's Trust. Sustare visits Rome and is honored by the Pope.

CHAPTER XII

Don's mansion is raided. Seven counts of contributing to the delinquency of a minor and two counts of sodomy are leveled against Don. John is able to buy up all the pictures, including those of himself and the Bishop. Don flees to California. A tacit agreement is reached with the D.A.'s office. Don will stay in California.

CHAPTER XIII

John claims that expenses incurred because of the raid have almost depleted the trust. Don's checks become smaller—his drinking gets greater. He dissolves in vodka. Months later he is admitted to a Charity Hospital. He expires in three days. The body is shipped to Boulder. It disappears mysteriously. An empty (closed) coffin is provided for the funeral. John does not attend.

CHAPTER XIV

Twenty years pass. John gets richer. Yage gets richer. The Bishop gets richer. John builds a huge golden bank in downtown Denver. The rectangular skyscraper is topped by a pyramid. Yage gives John some stolen Egyptian art to decorate his office at the apex. John becomes known as "Pharaoh John I."

CHAPTER XV

Bishop Sustare retires. Bishop Keel, his successor, demands that the trust which Bishop Sustare has so long held "for the Church" be turned over to the Church. The directors of the trust, John and Yage, refuse. There are suits and countersuits. The framework, built by Yage Thomas years before, stands. John and Yage control the trust. Sustare fears for his soul and decides to hand over the money. Yage runs down the elderly Bishop with his black Lincoln Continental.

CHAPTER XVI

Sister Mary St. John, unaware that the Bishop's death was not an accident, cleans out his safe. She discovers pictures of the Bishop and young boys from the raid twenty years ago. So the Bishop didn't secretly love her after all. She resolves to go to Bishop Keel with the documents and testimony that will break up Bishop Sustare's private trust. Yage Thomas, horny from killing the Bishop, picks up a young boy.

Extract from Chapter XVI

. . . to the Presidential suite of the Starlight. But first a kiss from those gumdrop lips. Yage turns to look at the boy in the blue light of the International House of Pancakes sign. The boy's face shimmers in the blue, he turns into someone or something else. Surely Yage can't expect otherwise. America is a media democracy—a land of shifting identities Where You Can Grow Up To Be President, a Heisenberg land. The face is steady now. It's the alcoholic face of Don Trampier. Strong dead hands close on the lawyer's neck. There has been a miscalculation.

CHAPTER XVII

Bishop Keel is able to retrieve the Church's money as well as all of the Trampier trust, which Bishop Sustare had been bagman for. Sister Mary St. John is shrived of her sins and retires to an old nun's home. John Rothe is publicly discredited and leaves Denver for his hometown of Carson City. There John discovers that he is the heir to Abramelin Rothe's estate.

Extract from Chapter XVII

. . . fit the gate, John wonders what the second key is for. A long heavy old-fashioned brass key, its barrel is decorated with kabbalistic signs . . . the garden is lovely. Rocky Mountain wild flowers abound. Fountains. The fruit trees

haven't budded, though. John moves to inspect them more closely. At the base of the first, a peach, is a small keyhole. John inserts the second key and begins winding the tree. When the spring feels taut, he pulls the key out. The tree buds, then blooms within a minute. John begins to walk to the next tree. Don taps him on the shoulder.

METAMORPHOSIS NO. 81

Harry got marked for a hot shot after the Rodwell brothers was busted. The word was that Harry had sold 'em out so he could stay on the street. Harry rode downtown. Everybody knew he was holding and three hours later he was tying up in the industrial green bathroom under the amphitheater in the park.

So the word got to the Violinist's place—he used to be in the symphony 'til he met the monkey—he supplied the Rodwell brothers and absorbed their clientele while they was away. And the Violinist decides that a stool pigeon should be singing to the angels. So he goes to a hardware store and buys some rat poison that's been on their shelf a hundred years—strychnine, bitter like junk, milk white in solution.

He soaks a paper sells it to Harry when Harry makes his Tuesday rounds to buy off the jones. After Harry leaves, the Violinist makes a pot of tea and calls his *companeros* to say that Harry Sladeck won't be 'round no more.

Harry goes to the public john where he keeps the spike almost at a run. What else could make a gray scarred old man like Harry move so fast?

In the john, Harry pops off the rectangular cap on a post that supports the walls between the seats. He takes out his works then goes to the little maintenance room where the toilet paper and powdered soap is stored. The lock rusted away years ago. Inside, an old gas water heater snores. Harry opens the little door on its side cooks up the H. Cooking with gas, Harry smiles. Throw the paper away filter the solution to get rid of talc or starch. Tie up and shoot.

As Harry walks up the stairs to the light, a burning heat crawls through his arm to his chest. Not the familiar warmth of junk—but hot like fire ants that day at his aunt's in Texas when the mower hit the nest. Christ burning and biting. Dark silver-greenbrown spots in front of his eyes. Terrific pressure he's being flattened out.

He falls at the top of the stairs on a bare patch of dirt packed by traffic sparkling with broken glass. He feels himself expand horizontally in time—a cone of light getting much larger . . . his body falls to pieces . . . a polar bear pisses on an ice floe . . . an African general warning his troops that the enemy practices necrophagy . . . a line of Russians waiting to buy toothpaste . . . everything falling apart . . . his junk-hungry body trying to return to the dust . . . a single drop of oil expands on a pond in rainbow arcs thinner, thinner and finally gone.

Far away, far below, at the head of concrete steps leading to a stinking john, grows a single opium poppy, blooming bright red in the February sunlight.

METAMORPHOSIS NO. 82

The practice of magic among the Marind-anim is based on dismay, by a grim despondency that choked his heart as a magic arrow. The coconut is the real source of death magic. Cruel, and momently the phantom was less and less the arrow is a serpent's head, with the arrow representing a serpent were less lovely, less subtle in their curves; the slender figure, plant juices, and with the exudate of a corpse.

The coconut must be shaped like a boar head because the neck an ordinary pallor. The soul of Malygris grew sick. The boar figures in these myths mainly as the animal hope. He could no longer believe in youth or beauty. Also a threat to human beings. The boar spirit is also connected with age, a thing that might or might not have been. There was usually represented as De-heroai, an old man with a long empty dark and the cold, and a clutching weight.

A boar ancestor who devastated the gardens day after day in accents that were thin and quavering like the ghost of its own liver and heart, pursued the killer. The fleeing men to dismiss a summoned phantom. The form of Nylissa come to me, the way a mother calls her child. He ran straight and surrounded her, was replaced by the last rays of the sun.

It Pays to Enrich Your Word Power

whaka-aro	Maori	To think upon, to consider the underside
aroa	Samoa	A chief's belly The child of a chief The seat of affection and feeling To be pregnant (of the chief's wife)
alo	Hawaii	Breast, belly
whaka-aro-rangi	Hawaii	To think about continually To love Brooding affection

We may add parenthetically:

(to) + (file) + (away) + (one's) + (head) + (with) + (someone)
= to make love

*

I had an awful experience once. It was like phantom lyrics; a period which I was unable to name despite my extensive knowledge. No door. That was before I had a name. Some people—surrounding tenements; and more than the dimness of the premature twilight . . . like a wild animal, those hypnagogic people. Drow Elves.

Or maybe I was born in the Garden of Eden and had no mother. In this premonitory dusk, through which all things were oddly distorted and assumed illusory proportions, I reached the house which was my destination. My father and mother wanted me to go to a place beyond the earth. But the house is mine and nobody can take it away from me.

And I am told that *mnophka*, the Venusian narcotic, is far worse in effects on the human system pressing against my back. The main trouble I have is too much speed or gravitation.

This is how the accident happened. I don't suppose you've ever heard of plutonium?

Dr. Manners rose from the pneumatic-cushioned chair in which he sat facing me, it was as if I were looking at myself. Dr. Manners began unscrewing the Anubis-head of the mock canopic jar.

This is not Alaska and the sundial is not sun dying, but I am afraid the sun will die. Manners was pouring snow from the jar, a drug from a Plutonian fungus. His nurse in virginal white robes (like a pelican before it tears its breast), Mizz Suzy Machworter, prepares the solution.

Dr. Manners lectures me on the purpose of the Plutonian drug in my rehabilitation:

"In the streets it's called the mirror-drug or the dopplerbuzz. The Elbslavs believe that the bride and the groom should not look back when going to church or both might die. Anyone who

129

kills a pig for a feast also has the right to have intercourse with the girl who nurtured and tended the pig . . ."

His voice drones on as Suzy pricks my upper arm. An image of a giant ice boar flashes before my eyes.

METAMORPHOSIS NO. 83

"That's your problem, nervousness about nothing," but he was writing "Librium 10 mg." He didn't know what it was like to be hunted.

FOEHN
HAMSIN
SANTA ANA

I leave the cool dry whitewall office for the hot parking lot. On the seat of my MG was burnt newspaper fireworms, still crawling, changing gray paper to white ash. Just the hint of a breeze. The car had been spotted. I walk by. Trying to act casual. The breeze picks up a little, five maybe ten miles per hour. Parking lot debris, mainly refuse from the BretonBurger down the block, begins to circle me. Bored Californians stare, tanned and isolated behind tinted glass, as I walk in the middle of a vortex.

A plastic garment bag lopes across the parking lot. A cross between an amoeba and a big friendly dog. Careful now, don't panic. The drugstore is still two blocks. Act natural.

The bag slides between my legs. Almost trips me. It's hard to pull away from my leg without trembling. I nonchalantly kick some loose pebbles on top of it, hoping it won't be caught up in the vortex.

Another quarter of a block without incident. Wind seems to die down; maybe I've fooled it. The real test will be crossing the street where the man-made canyon lets the wind blow strong and hard. Bernoulli effect.

I can hear the garment bag behind me flapping, trying to

break free.

The street now. Calm. Halfway across it hits me—a sixty, seventy mile gust pushes me a few feet.

"Ok. Dammit, Father, ok."

I remove my shirt spread my wings and take to the air.

METAMORPHOSIS NO. 84

I had a carving dream last knife. It was a beautiful knife full of stars and I was in a fashionable alley by the stage door canteen. And he came out of the canteen all tall and smelling of grease paint.

He walked down the alley past the dustbins and the graffiti swastikas. I was a small flower growing from a cement crack. A small blood-red tulip. And he bent over and picked the flower to grace his buttonhole. But the flower's petals were hard as steel and sharper than a surgeon's scalpel. His right hand bloomed with blood and he tried to fling the flower away.

But it clung, cutting into his palm so that the bone leading to his little finger was exposed. A mass of fine white filaments sprang from the blossom, covering his hand, absorbing the blood. He could feel the threads spreading through his bloodstream, an intense feeling unclassifiable as pleasure or pain.

Small holes appeared in his shirt and jeans as the bright steel buds of a thousand metal tulips sprang forth. And he bloomed like a burning man.

I call my florist and have a bouquet of red tulips sent to his dressing room. Tonight I'll wait by the stagedoor canteen.

METAMORPHOSIS NO. 85

For a gag Tom switched Hillary's pills. Now awake in the early morning, muttering and counting ceiling stains as the two amphetamines ride the saddle reserved for downers. Outside, below, each noise becomes a potential threat—a shuffling walk and Hillary will hold her breath—oh, God, don't let him hear me—the four-story elevation of her flat not withstanding.

About four-thirty Hillary notices the webbing in the corner. Barely swaying in the apartment's breeze, it might be shadow—no, it's webbing, it *casts* a shadow. Five minutes of trying to stare it away . . . ten. Close her eyes, seek sleep. Eyes open, five o'clock, the webbing has grown from ceiling to floor—spider can't sleep either.

A filament brushes Hillary. Webbing fills the clock. The wallpaper browns and curls at the edges. Hillary brushes another strand from her face. Oldwoman's hand. Wrinkled. Silver blue veins worming to burst free. She watches the golden watchband tarnish the white metal face, rust.

She wants to turn her head now but can't, it's held fast by thick ropy webs. Her legs sprout green and blue patches under the dusty negligee as the blood settles and the hemoglobin begins its complex decomposition. She hopes that her sight will also fail but it remains, strangely unconnected to the rotting of her flesh. Within seconds the weak fabric of her chair gives way, mingling her remains with the browning porous foam rubber.

By the time her bones have bleached and the wooden frame of the chair snapped with dry rot, Hillary has developed new senses, become aware of the others trapped in this room bleached the color of time. The actress clothed for the last black-and-white TV commercial floating by the bar . . . the three hippies in Army drag seated in lotus position around the crumbling remains of the stereo. Others less distinct . . . even a handlebar mustache cop from the 1890's . . . all look at her with pity and resignation.

All of the organics in the room have eroded into a glittering black dust about two inches deep. The inorganics and the tougher plastics have broken and weathered as though exposed to a million scouring October rains. Hillary rises and takes her place among the ghosts. A wind—from no apparent source—blows the ash into the ventilator ducts, leaving the parquet floor gleaming.

METAMORPHOSIS NO. 86

The procession of the ghostly window around the walls—the passing cars—the only stimulus that Rod had had for some hours. Mainly the window's image went clockwise in three broken arcs—the second of which illuminated Rod's pale face and dark hair at the height of its curve. The clockwise lights signalled the crowd leaving the stadium; the widdershins—usually moving slower—were old people returning cautiously to the college ghetto now that the excitement was over.

Rod ODed. Rod oded. OD.OD. 0

Rod broke into Dr. Wesson's lab at the beginning of the football game (when campus security became ill-equipped traffic cops). Dr. Wesson researched memory enhancement, particularly chemically enhanced learning. Years beyond Vassopressin. Dr. Wesson sneered at ACTH. Dr. Wesson had isolated a pituitary which activated the very symbols of the mind itself. Crawling thoughts with perfect memory. Thoughts which thought themselves. Grinning old alchemist. Rod saw this as the easy fix—grab a coupla pills and finally absorb those organic chemistry texts he'd avoided all semester.

Rod, strongly in the tradition of Dr. Frankenstein's movie assistant, took the wrong vial. Small blue tablets Dr. Wesson compounded for the primate research project at Cal Tech.

Heightened left-brain functions, particularly Brocca's area. Teach those monkeys to talk.

Rod took two of the tablets at eight-fifteen on an empty stomach. By eight-thirty they came on and Rod's language awareness began to increase to painful levels, creating vast Shandy-like discourses on the root of meaning:

I am going to get that book

think	liber	
therefore I have	to stand (sto, stare)	first
		r
I = eye	two	e
		e
am irregular verb	t̲o̲o̲	ALPHA gedden
		t
astigmatism	six	e
		x
		t

on organic chemistry.
off carbon indole rings   Kekule's snake
        diamonds are a girl's best friend
                herpophile

At midnight Rod imploded with a soft crash. Oroborous . . .

METAMORPHOSIS NO. 87

0

Marv the Gimp started an "overcoat" business. He apprenticed three human types—Eric Kustodiev, Jane Skal, and Davey Lorenz—as trapper-furriers.

I

UPI—Avant-garde sculptress Jane Skal is at it again. She's filling Nueva Austin with "traps"—oversize papier-mâché and plastic bear traps, drop cages, or spike pits. Every vacant dusty lot sports one of these huge gaudy sculptures. For "bait" she's using Monopoly money, mirrors, and cheap reproductions of collectible items (like 1804 silver dollars, or rare stamps). The "trap-series," she says, "symbolizes traps of attention and time in the modern world. Molechs and grinning idols with baleen teeth."

The source of funding for this ambitious entrapment of art is a subject of great speculation. The National Endowment for the Arts claims no responsibility.

Public reaction is somewhat mixed. The famous artists' colony of Nueva Austin buzzes with delight while the P.T.A. expresses doubts to the safety and taste of the project. Of particular worry to concerned parents is the automatic circuitry embedded in some of the traps. To add a degree of "artistic verisimilitude" certain traps close periodically. A roving van painted (on all sides) with Max Ernst's *Garden Airplane Traps* stops to service the sprung traps. Bearded youngmen under Ms. Skal's direction reset the trap, renew the bait, and admire the invisible catch in the best tradition of the Emperor's new clothes.

0

Marv the Gimp's boutique occupies a three-room suite on Park Avenue. It has no name no advertisements no notice on its mailbox. To find the boutique you need a certain greediness of spirit, a special light of desperation in your eyes. And you need to watch the signs: the break of surf at Coney Island, subtle changes in a radio static pattern, the pattern of leaf falls in Central Park.

Don't worry if you can afford Marv's prices. The Door to the shop will size you up. Only qualified customers may enter.

II

Eric Kustodiev, trapper and furrier, came into our lives with loud bawls of pain. Two nearly-parallel rusty barbed wire fences, marking two disagreeing surveys, separate my fifteen-acre retreat from my neighbors. Both fences gape with irregular holes and their posts lean in ill repair. At a narrow point where my fence posts lean toward Mr. Lowi's, Eric's large bottom and great belly were being simultaneously impaled.

As simultaneously—on the fifth yell I believe—Mr. Lowi and I were rushing forward with scissors, wire cutters, the iodine and the brandy (the brandy to cut the pain of the iodine, a customary pair locally). Mr. Lowi began applying brandy to the over-excited Kustodiev while I began freeing his posterior. As I removed the three barbed strands I wondered how such a large man could be stuck in such a narrow area. It was as though he had simply appeared there. Due to the course of later events I believe this to be the correct hypothesis.

Freed both posteriorly and anteriorly, Kustodiev downed the remainder of Lowi's brandy and reached for mine. After a brief consultation—wherein we agreed that the wounds should be carefully cleaned and dressed—we set off for Mr. Lowi's porch. I carried the large white box which contained the traps.

In the process of the cleaning and treating of Kustodiev's punctures more bottles of brandy were produced. Enough in fact that Eric flinched not at all when iodine was applied to his open flesh. I also drank enough brandy to ensure protection from future pains. The brandy substituted for the shared experience that creates friendships. I warmed to Kustodiev because he didn't know me. Twenty years a host for a local kiddy show, no one took me seriously on a first meeting. The salary was good hence the fifteen-acre retreat. The working conditions terrible (ever walk out of a liquor store next to a shopping mall and have some little kid point and yell, "It's Mr. Tobey Tomtit!"?) hence the need for the fifteen-acre retreat.

During the mellow haze, Lowi's daughter Kelly, eighteen, buxom, ruddy, blonde, waltzed by us carrying brown bags of groceries. Kustodiev fixed her with a look I'd seen on San Francisco Chinese jade merchants spotting a perfect carving.

Later still we granted our old friend Kustodiev right to trap in our wild truck gardens.

III

"I dunno what happened to the Hoff kid, officer. It don't got nothing to do with this joint. I've kept the Green Brain clean for years. No tricking in the john, no dope deals, no drag, no whoring. I work hard to keep it a respectable club.

"Look, mebbe it's like AIDS or sumpthin. None of the other cases were patrons here. They'll probably snap out of it anyway.

"Last guy I saw him with? Jeez, I don't know them all—no, it was that new guy, Davey El. I haven't seen him since either."

0

"It's absolutely *you.*"

II

The week following Kustodiev's appearance saw the shooting of five shows and an Easter special. I drove to my garden house overcome with fatigue. Kustodiev was making rapid rounds of his traps adjusting snares restocking bait. Lacking energy (or desire) to hail him, I slumped indoors to bed. A dream came—with such intricacy of detail and intensity that I knew it was dreaming. My garden retreat by moonlight, the flowers, ferns and weeds grown huge as in the lush rolling days of the Devonian. Kustodiev sat half-hidden in a blind, his red beard making him into Thor. Kelly Lowi, dressed as a nymph, moved to meet a shadow-hidden satyr.

She reached out to embrace—*snap,* the bear trap caught her ankle. She begged the satyr for help. I ran but Kustodiev was quicker. When I was five, maybe six yards away he'd grabbed her with a great hairy arm.

He scanned everywhere and spotted me. Something small and very very bright flickered in his free hand. Dazzled, I found myself back in my bedroom. At first I thought I was awake, standing looking down on my sleeping body. I felt something tug from my midsection and I was pulled into and around my body. I woke then feeling all bruised inside and several times more exhausted than when I drove home.

I intended to get up and check on my garden but fatigue overwhelmed intent. As I fell asleep I could hear Kustodiev singing an old Cossack hunting song.

The next day I learned that Kelly Lowi had suffered a cerebral hemorrhage in the night. Comatose, her recovery chances were rated at nil.

0

III

Tuesday evenings, Kustodiev went to Fat Dawgs from eight to closing. Then with crashing baritone echoes he checked his traps. He'd come to agreements with every landholder on U.S. 75 for nearly a three-mile stretch.

At 8:30 on Tuesday the 23rd I decided to check his bait. Crossing through one of the gaping holes in my fence and stepping over the corresponding low-hanging wires in Lowi's fence, I came upon a trap. Inside was the high school yearbook picture of Kelly Lowi. Good enough bait for Lowi or his wife (or me).

Gingerly, so as not to spring the trap, I removed Kelly's picture and placed it with the paper cutout of a satyr I'd found the night of Kelly's hemorrhage. I closed my wallet and replaced it, drawing forth an envelope from my shirt pocket.

Inside was a dated *Life* magazine photo of the Russian crown jewels. I placed the photo in the trap.

Wednesday morning I sat on a deck chair in my garden. I sat reviewing next week's scripts, watching a weary Kustodiev crawl into his pup tent.

Ninety minutes later the case trap sprung. Something small insectile and greenish—a nasty butterfly—struggled within.

IV

The tools necessary for curing stretching and sewing were in Kustodiev's tent. It took a week.

Slipping in and out of the thing's a squeeze. If I'm not careful it'll become permanently attached.

Now I can walk the streets stroking my full red Cossack
beard, my identity safely concealed.

METAMORPHOSIS NO. 88

He was a pretty kid with gray wolf eyes, that special kind of
beauty of a Genet hero. Fine white teeth except for the pro-
nounced canines, beautiful eyebrow growing clean across the
face, lycanthropy just beginning to set in. A great find for the
producer and a huge bonus for the scout.

Certain implants to maintain his feral beauty—they would
check the spread of the disease and keep him from coarsening
into manhood. There was to be no cracking of the voice, no
musculature deforming the throat, no fine black stubble on his
cheeks.

By seventeen he had "amassed" one of the greatest fortunes
in America. His face could be correctly identified by a Sene-
galese Gnaova musician, by a Bronx street fighter, by a Japanese Presbyterian minister. Not an article on his appetizing
person that did not contain the phrase "animal magnetism."

His album with back tracks of North American timber
wolves howling in heat conquered top ten for thirty weeks.

When he was nineteen he was quoted in world newspapers
giving sage opinions on peace, economics, environment.

Two years later comedians joked about his baby face and
high voice.

In another three years: "Boy, he was great, wasn't he?
Wonder where he is now?"

In a small back room at his record company . . .

On his thirtieth birthday the pressure of change tore through
ancient sutures—expelling implanted organs snapping and
elongating bones.

The werewolf slaughtered five before they shot him down.

METAMORPHOSIS NO. 89

A carnival fortune teller told me that travel was my destiny. I took the cards as a mandate. A small-town newspaper boy has strong spatial limits so I confined my travel to dreamrealms. For an atlas I had the faded yellowing copies of *Compleat Shakespeare*, my family's sole literary treasure. I can call spirits from the vasty deep . . .

Through the Invisible Doorway at night, leaving a body grown hard and cold as a rubber ball. I chose the land of the Moors where Cannibals did each other eat, the Anthropophagi, and men whose heads do grow beneath their shoulders. *Othello*, I, iii.

Standing in the blue sand of a lunar Sahara I see the approaching *ghuls* of the Great Sandy Waste. One gives a banshee call and I knew I am home. I run with the *ghul*-pack to the mountains whose tops are ever cloud-covered. There an ancient song raises a large limestone like a cork from the earth—its protective iron sigils glowing red under our magickal assault.

Darting into the secret city I cannot speak of what happens there. I will not betray my tribe. They forgive me my prodigal ways in Roumani Merikana: I eat the Prodigal's feast—flesh of Muslim slave traders and their cargo.

At the *ghul's* table all of my shadow life washes away save for one dream—a dream of my old body pliantly flowing into a *ghul's* body—deep in Illinois awaiting the alarum clock's crow.

Dandelions, being the principal flowering plant in the courtyard of my apartment, lead me to think often of dragons. In herbal innocence they recapitulate alchemical colors—black earth in December, white snow in January, green leaves in February, and gold blossoms in March. Two years I watched the dandelions telling allegories of Christian Rosykruz and Paracelsus missing the red dragon. Everything else an Adept could hope for was there—negrido, albedo, green lion, kingly gold.

The unchanging mercury in the blue lunar snow and tempestuous sulphur in the yellow light from the sodium vapor street lamp engendered the Egg in the dark earth between two rows of shotgun flats.

Eventually fire, the glowing red triangle, the Dragon, would come. Rene Thom, the French mathematician and discoverer of catastrophe theory, points out that human catastrophe leads to new human systems. I'd been looking at ground and sky and not at the peopled horizon.

I.N.R.I.

Igne Natura Renovatur Integra.

All Nature is renewed by fire.

Often a deep male voice denouncing his wife in English and Spanish interrupted my nightly meditations. Aren't Latins said to have a fiery temperament? Their mailbox gave me the clue to the Dragon's whereabouts. His name was Sam K. Nour. As any alchemist knows the Hebrew letter Samekh belongs to the plane of fire and Nour is the Hebrew "fire."

Having consecrated my sword, I waited.

On Friday night, as was the custom, my neighbor began beating his wife and smashing pottery. I left my apartment and forced the door to his. The Dragon had red scales and a toothed spinal ridge—lidless eyes of lambent yellow—crocodilian mouth—he grabbed the woman with two five-fingered claws, beating his purple wings to maintain his upright position. The

142

diamond spiked tail curled away under the TV set. The woman pounded on his jaws where the scales were smaller and presumably the flesh softer. I'd say the Dragon measured three meters.

I rushed in, bringing my vorpal blade just beneath the skull. A good gash, the room filled with the fetid odour of its ichor.

It turned and belched fire upon me, severely burning my left hand and shoulder. I drove my sword straight into its soft underbelly.

She called the police. How it changed into a man I do not know.

METAMORPHOSIS NO. 91

He wrote everyday because he was afraid that if he stopped he would forget how. His greatest fear was a sheet of paper covered in meaningless strings of words in his handwriting. Strings such as **TIME**

> **TOME**
> **COME**
> **COMB**

BOMB explodes suddenly outside. His garret shakes. The lights go out. He rises too swiftly. He trembles, regaining his breath. He walks slowly to the cabinet where the candles are kept behind the dishes. There is shouting below. He pulls out a white spiral taper and peels off its cellophane wrapper. He crumbles up the cellophane and drops the wad near but not in the yellow plastic trashbin.

He puts the candle in the wax-coated Chianti bottle near the typewriter. He walks into the other room. He stoops, opening the top drawer of the cherrywood nightstand. He fishes out a half-empty book of matches bearing the name of the workshop. He returns; lights the candle.

Someone or something whistles high and thin outside his garret window. He strokes an amulet under his stained T-shirt, and waits silently, holding his breath as long as possible. He shouldn't have lit the candle. Not today of all days.

Something moves away and he can breathe again. He closes the window. His heart is very loud. He takes long slow breathes, trying to remember the rhythm his guru had taught. One, two, in. One, two, three, four, hold. One, two, three **456**

656

666

366

365 died. He had written that on the last sheet. Had he meant the war? Or was he simply talking of a year's passing? He starts to cross out the notation, and paused with his stainless steel pen. Better to leave it. He intended to reread it all one day. Before he died. When he reread it he could die. He remembered the *Tibetan Book of the Dead* said that your life had to pass before your eyes before you entered the Great Void. Well he had it here. Or most of it. Some of the journals had been carried down the endless steps and across the tiny streets to the workshop. Sarah and he had stuffed them between the ceiling and the roof—laying them on the rotten insulation in the terrible winter of '93. He should go and get them before some rats or other vermin made nests in them.

The thought of the long trip—by foot—to the workshop depressed him. He decided to write a little, wait for the power to be restored. When he was a child he'd read about Tesla, who'd caused an incandescent bulb to glow simply by tapping the atmosphere. Tesla hoped to turn the whole earth into a giant battery and to capture the lightning. He had saved his pennies and written off to Edmund Scientific for Tesla coils and Jacob's ladders and so forth. For several months he'd been the wizard of electricity in his basement until he wound up electrocuting Mama's cat. Mama had few joys in life she had been **LAME**

LATE

MATE

had left him when he found Sarah. Joni had been a real witch from the Republic of Oregon. If she's alive she is probably back in Oregon. Serves her right, the winters are tougher there.

The light panel flickers. There's a brief cheer from the street, dying as quickly as the light.

Maybe he should write about Sarah

Sarah in sunlight
Sarah in darkness
Still Sarah
But who is Sarah when

Sarah goes away?

Sarah had been part of the drug revolution of '17. She had used the little yellow pills called logiazine. Logiazine changes the world map at the chemical level—it shuffles the deck. Sarah had come out of a forty-eight hour trip and walked out of the workshop past the main gate and was never seen again.

Sarah's last words were, "Of course." And he never knew if they were a soul-burning enlightenment or madness. He'd kept the pills for years, but finally flushed them away unable to follow.

(a whistle high and thin)

And then the electric light, a flicker, then full on. There were no crowd sounds. Perhaps they had all gone home. He was about to remember something about the crowd noises. Something not good. He was on the **VERGE**

VERSE
TERSE
"TENSE times," the guard had

said, last time he had seen the guard.

He blows out the candle. He opens the top drawer of the metal desk. He sees the blood-stained dagger. He slams the drawer. He closes his eyes. He braces for the whistle or the sound of claws on the glass. After many heartbeats he opens his eyes. His breath is short, his vision discolors with the systole/diastole of his pulse, and small silver balls boil before his eyes.

Color slowly returns to his ancient face. He opens his eyes

and reaches for the last few sheets he's written.

He can't hold the paper steady at first but by the third page he's calm. He picks up the stainless steel pen and makes a few corrections. He reads and rereads. He plugs the typewriter in. He hesitates before beginning to type. He glances at the window. It's late twilight. He unplugs the typewriter. He goes to the dirty kitchen to brew tea.

He uses yesterday's tea bags. The sugar bowl is empty. He reminds himself to make a note, and promptly forgets as he did yesterday and the day before. He feels better as the night comes on. He remains a creature of the night, even after all those years of trying to forget. He sips the weak hot tea. He remembers flying in the night long ago. He remembers the salve, the gestures, and then flight so long practiced in dreaming. He remembers the others that flew with him. He'd written a wonderful account of it in his magickal diary.

But the diary insulates the workshop. He wants that cutting memory. He'll go and get the diary, but after the tea.

After the tea he pulls his coat from the closet. He's surprised that it's dusty. He turns off the bedroom light. He wonders if he should bring his MSS to the workshop. Maybe he could read it to someone. He shakes his head and goes out the door. No need to lock it.

He walks a flight of stairs at a time. He pauses on each floor and rests. He's glad the lights still work. He tries to remember why he should be glad for such a commonplace occurrence. But he remembers his diary and continues. Down ten flights and into the lobby. No one's at the desk—no doormen either.

He walks out. There are no other buildings. A vast black shape blots out the stars as it flies overhead. He remembers
TAME
TOME
TIME

METAMORPHOSIS NO. 92

Our little Rose Window of our little village church began in 1959. Father Trampier took a pastoral retreat to the Algerian Sahara. To use the Desert (and be used by it) in the tradition of St. Anthony. The colonial officials smiled benignly on our Provincial priest. Red tape vanished like a water mirage. Father Trampier found a small oasis guarded by a few dates, visited by a truck or camel caravan once a month. An agreeable measure of hermitage for a modern man . . .

He erected a two-room shack with materials bought off the trucks. His bed raised on a platform of tires and his roof old tent cloths.

After erecting his shack the priest retired to the meditative life. At dawn he would rise, say his Office and begin his meditations. On the fifth day out he saw a peculiar glittering in the sand.

The glittering—at first almost imagination—would begin in a small patch and run through the spectrum from red to blue. The sequence took about 180 heartbeats, roughly two minutes. Then a nearby patch—seldom larger than Father Trampier's outspread fingers—would start. Sometimes two patches would iridesce simultaneously comprising a rough circle about sixty yards in diameter. Father Trampier dreamed of Irem, the City of Pillars, where the dead do not die but eternal lie. And dreaming . . .

An Arab family stopped to water their camels soon afterward. Father Trampier ventured to ask about the sand but either his Arabic was faulty or the subject taboo. In either case the family left and the oasis was not visited by locals again. The colonial trucks still stopped.

He gave a great deal of thought to the shining crystals. He concluded the light patterns were communication and even a sign of intelligence. With this conclusion he resolved to preach

Don Webb

to them like St. Francis to the birds.

The next day he began his readings to the glittering sand. He chose the opening of Genesis. As he spoke the crystals began flashing wildly. They rose in the air, whirling around the priest, entering his nose his eyes his mouth his ears. Sharp impacts cutting him deeply embedding in his bones.

He returned to our village in 1956.

Three years later he began to suffer sharp chest pains. One day in the bath he found a bright red line like blood just above his heart. Over the next few days a bright shard of colored glass emerged. He allowed it to develop until it caused a bulge in his cassock.

He went to the hardware store and bought a glass-cutting kit.

The shard came off easily—painlessly, like cutting nails or hair. He drew up the Rose Window from his dreams.

New pieces grew from his chest, one every few days.

He lost his hair, his nails stopped growing, as all of his body energy went into making the glass.

He passed on a few months after finishing the window.

A lovely thing when the light's right

METAMORPHOSIS NO. 93

fruitful—suddenly drawn onto the asphalt loop around the city built with DOD funds with visions of an asphalt-encircled glowing crater. Blue Cherenkov-effect gammas glowing on your retina—driving in hopes of awakening the Muse or at least gagging the yammering of frog-skin consciousness. Big white Chevy pickup—Mom, apple pie, all it needs is a gun rack.

Twice circled in widening gyre—meaning I drove in the slow lane the second time. No muse but gas consumption. I leave the loop for the Buddy Holly Park. The Bermuda grass

still tan and no ducks on the water.
Find a tree a good tree in this case a black-barked British elm
to sit by.
(("Why do you address a tree?"
"Because I am poor. If I were rich I would use a telephone."
Conversation between German parapsychologist and West
Indian woman circa 1943.))
I watch the future through the tree's shadow. A simple matter
of faces like watching your neighbors through a door's spy-
hole.
From the glowing blue crater (after images of the
Alchemist's Furnace?) the new men come. Covered with bright
scales, brown like roach chitin. They crawl from the atomic
blue and stare with little red eyes. Their eyes pose questions that
I can't answer.
I pull myself from meditation shaking away from horrible
shadows. I'm alone in the park. I stand, dust the tiny straws
from my backside. Walking to my pickup, I pick up a shiny
piece of green glass the shadows dropped—a tektite—silicon
with radioactive isotopes of beryllium and aluminum.
I pocket the green stone and drive home, hoping to incorpo-
rate it—like any dream-relic—into a charm of protection.

METAMORPHOSIS NO. 94

He was like a stage magician alla time directin your attention
to little bits of stage business. You could interview anybody in
this joint and they could tell you how he lit a match with only
one hand—bent from the book covered it—scraped—lit. But
not a single one of 'em could agree as to eye color or height.
Always trailin all kinda bad detective movie business—wore a
gray overcoat a nondescript rag hat had mysterious meets—
People walk inna bar hand him little notes or one guy done up

as a Mazori shaman comes in gives him a shark's tooth.
He specializes in trackin down the dear departed. You know
the line a friend or a lover in *Bardo* from AIDS or a car wreck
or cancer and you want to know if they made it to the Clear
Light of the Void or at least a good rebirth. So you hire him. He
went by *Rinpoche* but that's just Tibetan for Your Holiness or
sumpin.

Anyhoo, the night of the Schever wreck the bereaved family
comes in. Waits by his table. At eight as per usual he strolls in.
He orders a martini while they give him the tearful news and
where's-our-Johnny-now? bit.

So about eight-fifteen he goes into a trance and sez he sees
a red light. Atsa bad sign means Johnny's headed to an ignoble
womb.

Family begs him to warn Johnny off. He sez it's too late—
he can already hear lovemaking from the light, and it would be
too dangerous to get near it, and anyway Johnny's karma musta
earned it.

So the pinstripe-suit lawyer—Johnny's father no doubt—
offers him 2K cold cash to warn the kid. He sizes up the
pinstripe decides he's worth it and goes into trance. He begins
describing the Red Light and Christ! if you can't see it casting
shadows on his face. Whole bar quieted down then and we
could hear the fucking. And he sez I can't find Johnny. The
Light gets real intense and there's a sound like sucking eggs and
poof! he's gone. Just the clothes and hat in a pile by the table.
So I guess you're a few days too late or a few years too early
to contact him.

METAMORPHOSIS NO. 95

The last memory into the Rockin Robin for a drink and to see
Mr. Mesmero the stage hypnotist. Vague indistinct man, out-

lines blurring, making passes buzzing voices . . . then blackness. Nothing vague now, lying on a cold concrete floor smelling of oil and exhaust. A parking garage?

Susan sits up and yellow light blooms in her head. A concrete ceiling about three feet above the floor. She rubs her head, waiting for the impact lights to stop dancing through her brain. When the last dim blue amoeba swims before her she carefully moves on all fours playing blind man's bluff with her new environment.

A few feet behind her she discovers another prisoner. Dead? No, too hard—a mannequin, apparently a sportsman model. She traces his torso and then empty air where legs should be. Close by lay an arm and a bald sexless head.

After two subjective hours of crawling, Susan has discovered ten more mannequins and several arms and hands. Her prison apparently consists of an infinite dark plane three feet thick filled with discarded dummies. Some wore clothing.

A light. A glowing rectangle five feet wide and three feet tall appears about sixteen feet from Susan. Two figures on hands and knees pull a mannequin toward them. The light vanishes.

She crawls to the door, its afterimage floating in the dark above her. She clambers over four bodies and a pair of legs. She traces the doorway—wooden with metal hinges, five feet long, three feet tall surrounded by a cinder-block wall on either side and the concrete floor and ceiling. Susan tries to scream. There's a constriction in her throat, no doubt due to Mr. Mesmero's ministrations. Knocking brings no one.

No light comes through the door's cracks. Kicking a torso out of her way, she wriggles to the spot where the precious light will be.

Hungry, bored she falls asleep.

The light. The figures, two men in gray coveralls, pull her into a larger room. They quickly, efficiently unscrew her arms.

They bring her new arms—the paint had chipped on her old ones. They put her in an elevator up to the dressers.

Don Webb

Standing in front of the lingerie section, surrounded by admirers, Susan forgets her bad dreams.

METAMORPHOSIS NO. 96

No one had noticed crazy Al for years. So he walks up and down the roads and the alleys at night picking up debris. He don't hurt nobody and his er—rock garden I guess you'd call it—is far enough from any main roads not to be a community eyesore. The tree stumps were his latest craze.

Any stump that could be pried up from a vacant lot or from the backyards of more tolerant folk became Al's property. He'd lug 'em out to his slapdash house and set 'em real careful in a circle he'd paced out. Measured their placement with string and plumb line and well-worn copy of *Gregg's High School Trigonometry.*

You could see the craziness just in their layout. No symmetry, beauty or logical placement. Some bunched up, some spaced, some a few feet out of the circle. At first we thought it might be a sundial or maybe he'd got hold of a book on Stonehenge. But we could make no pattern of it.

Then the big May rain came, twelve inches in half as many hours. And ol Al ran around his stumps buck naked, hootin and hollerin, and some of the ladies of the Mary Martha Bible Class were driving by after church and called the sheriff to put an end to such heathen goings-on. So the sheriff locked Al up for a couple of days for creating a public nuisance and let on to the boys that it was just a few beers doing the dancing.

Well in June and July and these first two weeks of August it didn't rain. The cotton folks and the dryland wheat farmers had terrible losses which means all big capital business like furniture and appliances will hurt all year. And the round-the-house gardener watched his zinnias die and his tomatos put on little

152

scraggly balls—takes four just to make a mouthful. Somehow—and I suspect it was the eternal virgins of the Mary Martha Fossilized Hymen Bible Class—talk got started that Al was bewitchen the area. Fictitious genealogies (he was the grandson of an Indian shaman) or biographies (he's been to Egypt and you know what they say about mummies) generated around Al. At first I'll admit I retold some of these tall tales over a beer at the Texas Rose, but that's 'cause I thought of 'em as tall tales. But yesterday an effigy of Al was hung and burnt at the telephone pole nearest his house—guess they didn't want to get too close—and in black spray paint somebody wrote: Heathen Go Home! as if Al who's lived here since the war wasn't damn near a native.

So I took it on myself to visit Al's place by night—pick me a souvenir and mosey on back to the Texas Rose to show everybody Al weren't no bogeyman to be feared of. Al's a likeable old cuss and killing somebody for witchcraft's likely to give the community a bad name.

I walk into the stump circle. The ground's broken in huge clods just like everywhere. I pick up one and expose a yellow eye staring up at me. Part of a thin face. Someone buried? no, alive. I turn to run but the arms reach up all around the circle and pull me down into the dry hard earth.

METAMORPHOSIS NO. 97

the back lot scattering broken changing flowing images through the weeds and hunks of rusting metal each reflecting a metamorphosis . . . it is not too late to dream of other worlds . . . each shard a different image . . . flesh returning to Silly Putty . . . tadpole iterations of Bosch . . . can no longer hold the images together . . . changes outside of our focus . . . inside our focus . . . the mirror pieces shoot away faster than the speed of light.

153

Don Webb

The mirror vendor has left the back lot. He walks away. We see him in the distance, grown small by perspective. We return to sleep to change again. This time we

154